D0504808

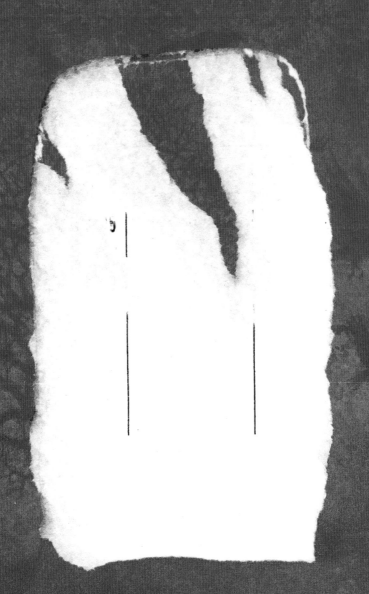

THE CROW CHRONICLES

The Mob

THE CROW CHRONICLES

The Mob

Clem Martini

BLOOMSBURY

Published in Great Britain in 2006 by Bloomsbury Publishing Plc
36 Soho Square, London, W1D 3QY

First published in Canada by Kids Can Press Ltd in 2004

Design by Ian Butterworth
Illustrations by Carol Lawson

A CIP catalogue record of this book is available from the British Library

Hardback ISBN 0 7475 7578 9
9 780747 575788
Export pbk ISBN 0 7475 8146 0
9 786747 581468

All papers used by Bloomsbury Publishing are natural, recyclable products made from
wood grown in well-managed forests. The manufacturing processes conform to the
environmental regulations of the country of origin.

Typeset by Dorchester Typesetting Group Ltd
Printed in Great Britain by Clays Ltd, St Ives Plc

1 3 5 7 9 10 8 6 4 2

www.thecrowchronicles.co.uk

To my wife, Cheryl, and my two daughters, Miranda and Chandra, who first inspired me to see the birds in the trees and then, as this new avian world opened up, completely embraced the Crows and came along for the whole ornithological extravaganza.

PART ONE

CHAPTER 1

Move in, everyone. If you can't see me, you probably can't hear me either, so move in. Move up the tree, move up the trunk, move closer on the branch.

Now, you all know me, or at least have heard of me. My name is Kalum ru Kurea ru Kinaar and I am old. Old. It's thirty-eight springs that I've gripped branch, thirty-eight springs that the land has weighed my shadow, thirty-eight springs I've tested and bested gales, spread wings and made my way north in thirty-eight tiring, trying, shoulder-wrenching migrations.

Some of you have been here wing to wing with me and lost feathers and bone in these troubles. Some of you were delayed, arrived late and have questions. Some have lost loved ones and, because you were separated, are only now learning of it. Move in. Move in and move up and you'll hear everything.

The sun has dropped into the final sixth on the horizon, and by custom it is time we began. Cousins, listen! A Gathering, a real Gathering is more than a simple reunion. A Gathering is a sacred, joyous and solemn occasion defined by ancient rules and obligations. It is the once-yearly opportunity for the Kinaar to assemble, recollect past events and make decisions. It is our time of lawmaking and law setting. It is a time when we recognize the passing of those who have completed the journey. It is only once we have added their names to the long record that their souls can leave the branch and fly satisfied to the Maker.

Now, you latecomers out on the edge, hush. All your questions will be answered. Those of you perched close, squeeze in and make room for those still setting down on the outer branches.

This particular Gathering has been unlike any other I have ever attended. The six great Clans of the Family Kinaar — Kemna, Kelk, Koorda, Kurea, Kark and Kush — have advised me, and I alone have learned everything that surrounds these tragic recent events. As Chooser, I have a duty to collect the separate strands of memory relayed to me, and from them weave the nest that will shelter and preserve our Family's history.

Now, all of you, rest your wing, still your fea[...] your beak. As is our custom, and with the blessin[...] Maker, I'll tell it to you as it happened, word fo[...] ...cred word.

I'll begin by saying that in all my thirty-eight springs, and all my thirty-eight winters, in all the time I have flown up the western seacoast, through the great midlands and here between the great northern plains and the forest, never have I seen such trouble strike the Family.

And experiencing that trouble was nearly the end of us.

CHAPTER 2

The day we set out, a driving rain blew out of the northeast. I felt an ache under my right wing as we took up and remember saying to myself, "This Gathering isn't going to be easy." Of course, I was right, but for all the wrong reasons.

Still, once that spring duster had spent itself, you could see the Family begin to dry out, fly out and find its wings, and by Great Crow, that's a glorious thing. We Crows are, after all, first and foremost creatures of the *air*. There's nothing that brings out the best in a Crow so much as these yearly migrations. They are nature's invitation to return to the element that first breathed us into being, the element the Maker made us for.

And as the clouds broke, the day became as sweet and fresh as ever there was. The scent of fish, flowers, seaweed and salt swept up from the ground. Backs warmed by degrees as a bright westerly sun burned off the remaining mist. We flew most of that afternoon, stopped to rest and feed at a deserted span of pebbly beach — tiny fish, blue-gray mussels and delicate, soft periwinkles — then continued up the coast.

The journey always seems daunting at the onset, but by the end of the first day, you begin to see the world differently — the wind lifting you, the ground dropping away. Earthly things a speck below. The ocean a span of blue and silver, glittering and dancing out to the edge of the horizon. This is the perspective a Crow was made for.

We were in no particular hurry. Flying with me were maybe two hundred souls, everyone in good order. Draped across the sky in our classic formation, we presented a long series of loose, cresting lines, maybe five or six deep, with two drop-backs and a head. Flying lead was Ketchum — at twenty-odd years old, he knows the way north like claws to his talon. Kyra to the left tip, Kark to the right. Immediately to my side, newlings Kora and Kek flailed away, firing up one draft, tucking their wings and hurtling down. Laughing and shouting to do it again. It made me tired just watching them.

Kyrk, however, wasn't inclined to be patient. He clacked

ak and delivered a withering glance in their direction. Blind in one eye, he never cared for things that jangled anywhere near him. He bunched up those powerful shoulders of his, leaned into an updraft and slithered right into Kek, blindsiding him. Kek tumbled through the air, head over tail, shedding feathers. A ripple of concern ran through the formation till Kek found his balance and silently dropped to the rear.

I drew up alongside Kyrk. I believe part of him already regretted what he'd done.

"What did you do that for?" I asked.

"You're in charge of formation," he growled. "You should know."

When I replied that it was beyond my understanding, he blustered some kind of nonsense about "lack of discipline" and "danger to the flock," then banked off right and took a position next to Kark on the tip.

It was early when we began looking for a place to spend the night. It's best not to drive anyone too hard that first day. We came to rest in a generous flowering plum tree with long, gnarly branches and smooth, silvery bark. The sun had only just slipped over the edge of the horizon and the sky was awash with color. Perched there among all those pink blossoms and their sweet-smelling fragrance, it was as if the sunset had actually descended into the tree.

The younger ones played in the updrafts off the ocean.

A few of the hungrier individuals flew to find forage. Most of the elderly settled in for quiet treetop conversation and a little rest. Klaryssa, the youngest in the flock, crouched on the branch next to me, head tucked in, exhausted. I was relishing the view — not performing Watch, Kymble was doing that — just looking, when I heard a low rumble above me. Kyrk again.

Had I, he wanted to know, put my mind to the security of this location? He fixed that one beady good eye on me. "There's a human roost," he continued, "only a short distance up the coast."

I'd seen it, I told him. A shabby, crooked arrangement as abandoned as a four-stick nest. That wasn't enough for Kyrk. He asked if I had actually checked it. Well, he knew I hadn't. We'd all just found roost.

"It's all very well to think it *looks* abandoned," he pressed, and I could tell he wasn't just talking to me but over me, to others in the tree. "*Looks* abandoned. Anything can *look* abandoned — until humans tumble out with their stingers."

I felt my feathers rise. "Go!" I told him. "*Go* and *check* for yourself if you're that concerned."

Kyrk clacked his beak at me. He had not *chosen* this roost, he reminded me. *I* was Chooser. *I* chose the route. *I* chose the roost. *I* was responsible for matters of security.

My wing ached, but I could tell that he'd go on all night if I didn't do something. Tired as I was, I was prepared to go when Kyp appeared. He would perform reconnaissance, he declared. I hesitated as I saw all too clearly the trouble that presented — then accepted when I realized that the offer was already made and there was no avoiding the trouble. Kyp launched off the branch in that peculiar jump, hitch way he's perfected and swooped off in the direction of the human roost.

I'd given the human's roost the once-over when we'd flown by it. Like most of their shelters, it was square, with those smaller openings on each side and two larger openings at ground level. But the color had faded, the framework sagged, and the grassy area in front was unkempt and unwatered. Nor was there any sign of the moving boxes humans fire about in, and that's pretty much a giveaway that the human isn't around.

There was a time when the migration would pass day upon day and you'd not see a human or a sign of a human. Now, it's keep your head up all the time. Each year there are more and more Outcasts and Stay-at-Homers — individual Crows who don't migrate, who don't follow the rules or the old ways. They stay where humans stay, eat what humans eat and, in many ways, have more in common with humans than with Crows. The rules were created to protect us, but this brood has hatched in a time when it seems there are countless ways to break the law. Each year so many young Crows are expelled — twenty from within the Kinaar in the past year! Twelve last year from the Kemna alone, and eight between the Koorda and the Kush. What will happen when there are more cast out than kept in? What use is purity if we are shattered and scattered? I suddenly felt a wave of impatience sweep through me.

"That roost isn't inhabited now, and I would bet it hasn't been inhabited for years," I said irritably. Kyrk sat still as stone, as if I hadn't said a word. We waited. I sighed and shifted from one leg to another.

"That new one who joined us today. That big fellow," Kyrk said abruptly.

"Kuper?"

"Yes, that one. What Clan does he eat with?"

I glanced over at Kyrk, but he didn't give away anything. It's hard to know what he's thinking sometimes. "He's Kerra's great-nephew, from farther south."

"Kerra's folk," he repeated, as if tasting the name on the tip of his beak. "Kemna, then. Was he Outcast?"

"No."

"Where are his parents, then, and those of the nest?"

"Dead. He's flown solo these past few years."

Kyrk gave a restless toss of his shoulders.

"You don't like that?" I asked.

"No," he groused, "and I don't like *him*. He took his time before declaring."

"Dead, Kyrk. All his nest-family, from the trunk out."

I looked straight at Kyrk. I couldn't understand what had so gotten under his feathers. "You *know* there are no humans at that roost."

He glanced off in the direction of the ocean, and for a moment all we did was listen to the surf sucking and slurping in the distance. I couldn't tell if there was something he was watching or whether he was simply refusing to look at me. "Maybe not," he said finally. "But how will newlings understand the need for vigilance and attendance on custom if you don't model it?"

There it was again, his doubts about my ability to lead. By all rights, Kyrk should have been selected as Chooser. My elder by two years, Kyrk has always been larger and stronger than me. His plumage has always been dark and rich — almost blue black — and regardless of the weather, he's always well groomed. Since I turned thirty, I've put on weight. No matter how I preen, I find I look a little wind-blown. For whatever reason, maybe only because I make the rest of the flock look good by comparison, I was selected to Choose six years ago, when our previous Chooser, Kendra, met the Maker following an encounter with a falcon. Kyrk was never able to rest easy with that decision.

I felt the branch sag, turned and saw Kyp just folding his wings. It was safe, he reported, the human roost abandoned, all its entrances open to the elements.

"Are you certain?" Kyrk interrupted, staring hard at Kyp. "Did you inspect according to law and custom? Unless three circuits around the object have been completed —"

"I flew inside," Kyp interrupted.

"Inside?" Kyrk repeated.

"Yes."

I knew that Kyrk was surprised, but when he spoke again, he had regained his composure. "I see. Of course, it will be necessary for you to perform purification then."

"It's late," I objected.

"The law is clear: after close contact, purification is required."

I opened my beak to protest further but Kyp interrupted me. "I don't mind doing it," he said calmly, then gazed directly at Kyrk. "It's just another rule."

"Certainly," Kyrk continued, frost under every word, "and by attending to these rules, each rule, we maintain the legacy passed down to us by our ancestors. So? You will purify yourself now?"

"Of course," Kyp replied evenly.

"Satisfied?" I asked Kyrk.

"The safety of the flock according to custom will always satisfy me. Nothing more," he replied in that rumbling voice of his. And then, as he flew off, "And nothing less."

I turned to Kyp. "You actually flew *inside*?"

"A quick pass," he admitted.

"That was unnecessary," I said, and shook my head disapprovingly. "And dangerous. Who knows what roosts in there now!"

"I didn't linger. And the three circuits wouldn't have been enough for him. Kyrk still would have found something to criticize," Kyp said, and then whet his beak against a tree branch. "The safety of the flock will always satisfy me," he mimicked. "Nothing more and nothing less." He snorted. "*Nothing* satisfies his bunch. And it's not so much safety that they're interested in as it is 'attending to the rules.' How can you listen?"

"It's my job," I said, shifting my weight to ease my hip, "to listen."

"But why?" he asked. "*You're* the Chooser."

"Being Chooser means a lot less and a lot more than you think."

"Just so you know," Kyp said, then he lowered his voice, "most of us younger ones are on your side."

I lowered my voice. "Just so *you* know — it's not about sides. Choosing means making every member of the flock feel each decision made was *their* choice. And that means respecting opinions, even when you disagree. So watch what you say and understand that *he* has influence enough to make life extremely difficult for you if ever he puts his mind to it."

Kyp laughed, kicked off the branch and sped into the

dusk. "Don't worry!" he called back over his shoulder. "I'm not about to do anything stupid."

"Don't worry?" I must have sighed heavily because little Klaryssa woke briefly before settling back down. I did worry. I worried because I knew what a long memory Kyrk had. I worried because I knew that Kyrk still had a dedicated following, especially among the Kurea and Kush. I worried because I knew just how close the Family was to a Splitting. And I worried because Kyp's last remark was just the thing someone said before he did something stupid.

I squinted up at Kyp, gliding in the tight, precise circles of prayer and purification, and then at Kyrk, high in the tree, and sighed again. Slowly, a silence descended. My forewings ached right up through the breastbone. I leaned against a spray of pink blossoms, inhaled their fragrance, tucked my head under my right wing and went to sleep.

CHAPTER 3

A clear, cold spring welled up from a rough sandstone outcropping not far from the seashore. After sunrise, a few of us decided to take a quick dip. There's continuing debate about whether this is proper behavior. Certainly it's not *safe* to bathe where the water is too swift or deep. A Crow is a Crow after all, and I'm not advocating a long swim. But where it's safe and practical, I hold that it's refreshing and good to duck entirely under the water and let it wash over wings, crest and crown. I did so, had a final deep drink, then, still dripping, we set out.

As the day wore on, our numbers increased. Kelty and her bunch joined us not long after we'd started — about twenty-five in all, and all tiny bodied and serious minded like

Kelty. They slipped into formation so silently it was several moments before they were noticed. Kyrta and two other families — forty individuals in total — appeared all at once over a hill just after midday. Kyrta has a huge voice and a booming laugh, and small talk and chitchat could be heard filtering up and down the flock for the rest of the day as we flew. That's always been a major part of what I enjoy about the Gathering. The closer you get to the Tree, the more familiar faces appear. "Good eating!" someone will call, and you'll glance over and see several dark bodies winging your way. "Good eating!" someone else will reply. Crows fall in and the flock moves on, that much larger.

Of course, opportunities for collecting really juicy gossip increase with every stage of the journey. Everything that's been said or done during the past year gradually filters through the flock. Ripples of excitement or outrage work their way from one end of the group to the other with each new discharge of information.

We skirted the coast for three more days, then banked east and began to work our way through a high mountain pass. What with your berries and fish and the like, the coastal route always provides plenty of good eating. For sheer joy of flying, though, nothing compares with tearing through the mountains. Enormous temperature changes accompany each rise in elevation, so the air masses shift from one valley to the next. A small breeze in one valley, funneled through those tight mountain channels, becomes a bucking, bracing blast at the other end. Snag the right draft and it will carry you higher than the highest peak — just tuck in your wings and hold on!

If the weather permits, it's traditional to stop and allow younger ones who still have the wings to compete in the games of flight. The games are an ancient tradition from First Times, when Kana-First-Hatched of the First Brood snatched fish from the outstretched talons of Sun Eagle. That began the Long Chase, which lasted one hundred days and nights. When we watch our youngsters fly, we celebrate the Crow who flew the feathers off the Eagle Family. Over the past few generations, though, I've seen the young ones apply themselves with an intensity that didn't exist in my generation, and they are certainly more adept than we were. They fly like no other Crow ever has. Among the Kinaar are individuals — Ketta and her brother Kory, Karl, Kesky and most especially Kyp — who can transform the act of flight into poetry. Nothing is quite so thrilling now as watching these younger Crows practice that most ancient and honorable art.

Crows aren't your fastest fliers — your hawks and falcons fly faster. Nor do we fly the farthest — geese and terns both make longer migrations. But is there any bird that can fly more sweetly than a Crow? Any bird more agile? Any other bird that can gauge the wind, test it, find its weight, play it and tease it and ride it like a Crow? We Crows are pilots of the wind, acrobats of the air, placed on Earth by the Maker to measure each gust, each breath — and in *this* we have no equal. Let hawks and terns reign in matters of speed and endurance — when Crows fly, we fly with *style*.

It took four more days to wend eastward through the mountains. At this point in the migration, muscles tighten up, fatigue sets in and tempers rise. We encountered a bit of a set-to over whether to make a certain rest stop. Kyrta received a tip from some more or less friendly ravens regarding the location of a hot spring. Some — notably Kyrk, Kork and Ketch — were of the opinion that any information received from ravens was suspect and should be disregarded. Others — and I found myself in that camp — felt that after the rigors of the migration, a hot soak might be just the thing. I felt if Kyrta had persuaded ravens (a notoriously dour, tight-beaked bunch) to divulge a useful bit of information — well, good for him.

But how does the old saying go? "Nothing so simple that temper can't complicate." The level of debate grew very heated, very quickly. Ketch — renowned for his hearty dislike of both ravens and baths — declared that all ravens and raven sympathizers should form their own hot-water-loving tribe and push off. Kyrta argued that anyone who didn't have the common sense or courtesy to accept a gift — from ravens, magpies or *who*ever — had a soul so shriveled and puckered that a soak in a hot pool was exactly what was needed.

As it turned out, the Hot Soakers prevailed.

High above the tree line, we came upon a spooky, craggy landscape dotted with the occasional snow patch. The spring emerged, as the ravens had said it would, meandering down the mountainside in the prettiest feathery cascades you've ever seen.

We set down in a rocky dimple in an immense boulder-strewn scree slope. The lake was clear to its stony bottom and rimmed with delicate tendrils of steam. Its source was a jagged-lipped, ominous-seeming black cave on the north shore. Out of this dark slash gushed jets of scalding water.

From our earliest days, we're taught to stay well clear of all caves — holes, burrows, tunnels and whatnot — as these offer homes to the manner of creatures that Crows want nothing to do with. As Chooser, I had the responsibility of making the final judgment. I flew as close as I felt comfortable to the cavern's mouth. Slick, sweating gray walls greeted me. A thick, green, mossy carpet ran along the ground before an impenetrable dripping gloom. Warm, wet, pungent air enveloped me, like the exhaled breath of the earth.

As I stared into the darkness, a strange chill ran through me. I hopped closer. Listened harder. These warnings generally mean something, but I couldn't see anything untoward, so after I had lingered longer than I should have and given the challenge a number of times, I delivered the All Clear. One after another, the flock descended.

The smell of sulfur was intense. To the windward side of the pool — nearest the cave entrance — my eyes watered. The water itself, however, couldn't have felt finer. Hot enough to turn your beak pink, it was warm and delicious after a few moments. Soaking in the shallows, I felt the water melting away all aches, pains and cares of the migration. I remembered an old story I'd heard from my ancient Aunty Keeta of a pool that restored youth to every bird that landed and bathed in its waters. Although they intended to stay only a short while, the birds were seduced by their increasing youth until at last they reverted to an egg. That magical pool, Aunty said, was lined with what appeared to be round boulders, but were actually thousands and thousands of eggs — the remains of all the birds who had received more youth than they had bargained for. Be careful, warned Aunty, what you wish for.

I wondered if we too might be so transformed. Feeling warm and lazy, I'd half decided that wouldn't be so bad. In any case, although we were not made any younger, we did stay later than we should have — and I note that some of those most inclined to complain of the delay earlier were *last* to get out — making it impossible to travel much farther because of the fading light.

Instead of pushing on into the next valley, we simply dropped down the mountain slope until we came upon a sheltered glade of thin, knobby alpine larch. The journey's rigors, combined with the torpor of the sulfur waters, produced a sudden irresistible fatigue. The Family hugged those larches, swaying in the mountain breezes, and we all drifted to sleep almost without saying a word.

In the dark, rocked by mountain winds, I dreamed the Story as it has gone since First Times. Long ago, Great Crow was large as a tree, and trees were large as mountains, and mountains stretched to the stars.

At the talon end of the mountains, in the most remote hole, lived Badger. Not Badger as we know badgers now. This was First Time Badger — solid as a hill, long clawed and always hungry. Badger, who couldn't fly or climb a tree, heard a sound one day as he dug. He craned his shaggy flat head, squinted up into the far-off sky and saw Great Crow soaring. Badger felt a stab deep inside his wretched soul. He felt jealousy. His long tapered nose and wide, furry brow wrinkled, and a low growl rumbled from deep in his belly. He stared long after Great Crow had disappeared and made a vow that he would rid the world of the creature that made his immense self feel so small.

That night, while all the world slept, Badger convened a secret meeting. His cousin, Pine Marten, is skinnier than Badger and has smaller teeth and claws, but he can slip up a tree quick as a squirrel. Badger convinced Pine Marten to search out the nest of Great Crow and his mate and steal their brood. Pine Marten waited until Great Crow flew to find food, then crept up to the nest and sang Great Crow's mate to sleep. Six eggs, green gray, oval and delicate, were carried away by Pine Marten.

Day came. Sun rose. Great Crow returned. He saw the empty nest, and a terrible despair seized him. He and his mate wept. Great Crow flew to each corner of the world, searching. "Have you seen my eggs?" he asked.

Eventually the rocks showed pity. As the wind slid through their cracks and crannies, whispers rose that Pine Marten had stolen the eggs and Badger had hidden them. Quickly Great Crow flew to the entrance to Badger's den. Grim remains littered the ground — bones, beaks, feathers and skulls. Great Crow called to Badger, "Come out!"

From under the earth, Badger's gravelly voice rumbled, "What do you want?"

"My eggs," called Great Crow. "Return my eggs."

From within the heavy gloom of that tunnel, Great Crow could see two small lights — Badger's tiny red-rimmed eyes. "What will you give me?" whispered Badger.

"My talons," answered Great Crow.

Dirt and dust rose from the cave's mouth as Badger dug deeper. "I cannot return your eggs," called Badger from a more distant part of his lair, his voice fainter.

"My beak, take my beak," called Great Crow.

Came a still more distant reply, "I cannot return your eggs."

"My wings," called Great Crow, unfurling his most prized possessions.

"I cannot return your eggs," said Badger, his voice so faint that it was almost no sound at all.

Finally, Great Crow said in a quiet voice, "All of me."

A stillness stretched tight over the valley as Great Crow waited, and all the creatures of creation waited, listening.

Then Badger said, "Take them."

Great Crow gathered his brood, gently, and placed them up high, high on the hidden limb of the tallest tree at the farthest edge of the world, where his mate warmed and cared for them. He sang mighty spells round them so no creature could find them, neither with sight, nor smell. Then he returned to the dark cavern. He stepped over the debris, lay himself down on the dusty floor and closed his eyes. Then Badger crawled up from his deep pit and devoured Great Crow — legs and wings, tail and crown.

For five days, Great Crow was nowhere to be seen, and all the world wept. Where was flight to be found like that of Great Crow's? Where was laughter to be heard as infectious as Great Crow's? Who could spin stories or tell jokes like Great Crow?

On the sixth day, though, a miraculous thing happened.

A great noise was heard, like the cracking of the sky, which itself is but a shell containing and protecting all the world. In that nest on that tree at the edge of Earth, one of the sacred eggs shattered and its delicate shell fell away, but instead of a small, blind, featherless hatchling, Great Crow emerged full grown and shook himself and flew. Reborn.

When I awoke from that dream, it was early, early morning. Only the faintest orange glimmering outlined the upraised silhouettes of the peaks in the east. The rank breath of Badger still scorched my beak, and the memory of the cavern so far beneath the ground made me shudder.

The story of Badger and Great Crow is sacred. A dream of that kind never appeared without a reason. On that branch in the frosty morning, I could only wonder, why *that* dream? What was the Maker trying to tell me?

CHAPTER 4

The next day, we abandoned the craggy mountains, hot springs and piney forests as we steadily dropped in elevation. On the far eastern side of the range, the great plains opened up, and there we turned due north.

Klayton and his bunch joined us, increasing our numbers considerably. The prevailing winds urged us on from the south and west, so we had the breeze at our backs and consequently picked up speed. Within three days, we'd reached the outskirts of that sprawling human rookery that surrounds the Gathering Tree. At that point we numbered upward of eight hundred.

The human habitations nearest the Gathering Tree first appear as a series of small, isolated constructions. Then the roosts grow closer and closer together, and the paths laid out by humans become choked full of those fast-moving, smoke-spewing boxes humans travel in. Suddenly, on the horizon, human roosts rear up, tall as small mountains and sharp edged, glittering in the sun like upright icicles. At night these structures glow and wink as if they housed a thousand stars. Taken all together, they're amazing things.

Now, humans are trouble, and are our rivals from First Times, but they also share many admirable traits with Crows. Like Crows, humans appear to mate for life and gather in groups for the sheer enjoyment of company. And like Crows, humans seem to share some form of communication.

I've often wondered if there aren't different *types* of humans — as there are different types of insects. How else can you explain humans who dwell in small, squat wooden roosts, and these others who erect towering columns of polished rock? I put this question to Kaleb, who has done some traveling, and he says that in some far-off places *ants* build towers and live in them. Sometimes as I fly, I'll look down at humans doing whatever they're doing — hurrying somewhere, hauling something. Busy, busy, busy. Just like ants. And from high in the air, there's nothing they resemble so much as *ants*. So, maybe there's more connection between your ants and humans than one might at first believe. But that's just one Crow's theory, and I haven't done any hard thinking about it. I will leave it to the younger generation to investigate.

Some birds find these towering structures fine places to nest. You can spot pigeons and gulls there most any time. However, more and more lately you're as likely to find hawks or falcons sweeping the air between these spires, and a peregrine can cut a Crow out of a flock faster than you can say "Good eating," so I tend to steer clear.

Instead, I led the clan along the river valley that bypasses the heaviest concentrations of human settlement. Zigzagging with each bend and twist of the river, we finally arrived at the limestone cliffs that announce the final approach for our Gathering.

I spiraled up a thermal that rose off the cliff facings, and there it was — the Gathering Tree — like an immense green fountain spraying up out of a sea of swaying grasses. I felt that same catch in my throat that I do each year when I see the Tree for the first time. We'd arrived.

CHAPTER 5

A Gathering Tree isn't chosen lightly. It first has to be proven. It must be large — each year hundreds of our folk convene and roost in its branches. It must have adequate food nearby — hundreds must find forage within a few moments' flight. It must be recognizable — newcomers should be able to find it readily. The branches must emerge high enough on the trunk to discourage your cats and raccoons, martens and fishers. It must stand out on its own, away from other trees, so we can safely watch for owls and hawks — and humans.

Our Gathering Tree was selected twelve generations back by Klara the Eldest and was a big, towering tree even then. Since its choosing, I'd heard many stories about it.

How Klara first spied it from a great distance, silhouetted against the setting sun like an enormous Crow perched upon the limestone cliffs. How it had brought our Family good luck and good eating. How even on that very first day of choosing, when it is customary for the Chooser to insert some small gift — a feather or seed or berry — into the bark of the Gathering Tree, Klara discovered a lily-white freshwater pearl in the river. She inserted it into the tree's folds, a special sign of blessing upon it and the Kinaar. (Since then, how many newlings have spent long afternoons searching the tree for that pearl?) A towering cottonwood with immense sloping branches, the tree had roots that twisted and curled around the crest of those white stone cliffs.

I recall as a chick crouching safely in this tree's shelter. I remember staring with wonder at the grasslands stretching yellow and tan on one side, the mountains etched purple against a pale blue dome on the other. The tree seemed to reach up and support the very edges of the sky.

Over time, humans crept closer to the tree, and where humans roost, they stick like pine gum. Today their sprawling roosts edge to the very crest of the hill. Human paths and human roosts stretch off in all directions, except on the cliff side. Still, the tree had been left some breathing room and a splendid view over the valley.

Now, I'll tell you something — this tree held special

memories for me. I recollect the familiar sharp smell of sap rising in spring and the soft, raspy chuckling its branches made when a breeze blew up. I've watched the bark toughen and roughen and thicken over the years and can remember individual roots stretching and rearing through the grass, like talons reaching out to more firmly grip the soil. I can recall all the Family it's nurtured, all the hurts it's healed, all the generations it's protected and shaded and sheltered. My great-great-grandfather was born in this tree. My mother met my father in this tree, and I first courted my late wife among the tall grasses in its shade. This tree, this big old tree.

I perched near its crown. The branch bobbled under my weight, exactly as it had a hundred times before. I felt a whir through my breast and had to take a moment to calm the rush of emotions. Then I summoned the Family, and over nine hundred Crows settled — preening, chatting, cooling themselves.

The clatter of Crow calling to Crow — is there anywhere a friendlier, happier sound? All the introductions and reintroductions. Newlings presented for the first time to great-aunts. Gossip being exchanged. The first moment of the first day of the Gathering had begun, and it was anticipated that another four to six hundred Crows were still to come.

We had been unusually lucky. Spring promised us good

eating of an extraordinary variety. Bugs were already out. Earthworms. Normally when we arrive, the Awakening has barely commenced, but this year it was already in full bloom. Speckled tadpoles in the slough at the bottom of the cliffs. Tiny grasshoppers, crunchy as nuts, clinging to grass blades. Gnats, and midges, and mosquitoes. Ground squirrels and gophers, mice, voles, shrews and salamanders. The humans' great cache of food — just a few hills over — was always full of good salvage and was replenished daily. And of course when it warms, humans gather under the open sky to burn their food. If a Crow is quick or a human careless — and we are as surely as they are — additional treats can be had.

In every way, that first day of the Gathering was about as perfect as could have been asked for. It should have been one of the finest Gatherings ever. How quickly things can go wrong.

Forgive me. I must take a short break. I'm sure all this talk of food has made you hungry. There's still some light in the west to forage by, and we've perched long enough.

CHAPTER 6

Everyone fed? Stretched? Anyone take a dip in the anthill? Let me tell you, an ant bath is one of life's great and decadent luxuries. These smaller black ants get to all the places that can't be reached by beak or claw. Stretch out over a nest, dust yourself all over, and pretty soon they're roaming up and down your body, nibbling and snacking, scouring all those difficult-to-reach areas, picking out the ticks and mites and satisfying itches that couldn't be satisfied otherwise. A glorious sensation! Of course, while you lie there, you're vulnerable, so make sure you post backup.

So, where was I? The Telling.

I have a confession to make. The Telling is always more

important than the concerns of any individual, because the Telling is the collective story of the entire Family, but in this case the story is in part the story of my own failure. The troubles that came upon us have been a long time in coming, and there were signs that a more capable Chooser might have read. It's painful for me to say this. Had I been more fully awake, more truly aware, perhaps I would have seen the signs and then much of the trouble could have been avoided.

I have been telling you how things have changed over the years that we have met at the Gathering Tree. The proximity of humans has been one of the biggest changes. Humans encroached on the tree from three sides, and with humans come all nature of their servants and slaves. Their dogs don't present any particular danger. Oh, they'll bark and fuss round the base of the tree with their tongues dangling, showing their teeth and scaring the newlings — but has there ever been a dog quick or smart enough to catch a Crow? Never has been, never will be.

Cats are another story.

Cats of any kind are trouble. Now, not all your cats are dangerous. I would venture that not even most are. There are plenty who are too lazy to run and too fat to stalk. But there was one who lived near our Gathering Tree who had to be watched. This cat, a sandy and copper mix, we called the Red One or, for short, the Red. Big through the shoulders and thick furred, hefty without losing a bit of agility, he had gold, hard, penetrating eyes.

More than any other cat I have ever seen, the Red had an appetite for birds. Many times over the years, I've seen him crouch still as stone in the long grass by the edge of the ravine, waiting for robins, starlings or any of the littler birds. Many times he flattened himself beneath trees, or in the shadows of the thorny caragana bushes, and silently eyed the nuthatches, waxwings and grosbeaks. And once — in years past — he caught a Crow. Kif ru Kush in the Year of the Half Darkness.

Whenever any of the Kinaar spied him, someone would send up the Call, and the Red would crane his furry head, twitch his long orange tail and stare with those flat, cold, golden eyes. I don't know what kind of thoughts cats have, but I'm sure that in those moments they weren't charitable ones.

Kyp alone in the flock seemed to have no fear of the Red, in a way that you could see was a little reckless — but then, what youth isn't reckless? Caution comes with wisdom. Wisdom with experience. Experience with age.

In any case, Kyp had developed a reckless game. He would forage in a grassy stretch very near where the Red was known to hunt, giving every impression that he was completely, totally involved in his search for seeds and bugs. His head dropped, his tail rose. His eyes remained fixed on the ground. He never once scanned the sky or glanced from side to side. For all intents and purposes, he was a Crow totally without defenses.

If Kyp continued in this manner long enough, eventually the Red would appear. Nothing would herald his entrance; he'd simply *be there*, like a phantom — just a whisper at the base of the bushes. Slowly, the Red would creep closer. Slowly — so slowly that no single movement was actually seen — he would slither forward until he crouched at the very edge of the shadows. Then he would explode. In a blur of legs and lashing tail, he would fling himself at Kyp, legs and body uncoiled, mouth agape, claws unsheathed.

And at that precise moment, Kyp would hop and lift into the air, *juuust* beyond reach. The enraged Red would grasp air and fall gracelessly to the ground, hissing and spitting. Kyp would fly in lazy circles above, laughing. Everyone watching from the neighboring trees would explode into laughter as well.

When the game went right, the laughter continued through the day. There was always plenty of humor in the humiliation of the Red. I mean, what Crow doesn't relish seeing a cat cheated of dinner? And there was joy and appreciation of the prowess Kyp displayed — after all, Kyp's timing and control were incredible. And there was laughter — and this was rarely admitted — from sheer relief. Because each time Kyp set down on that grass, each time he exposed his back and let the Red stalk him, each time that flurry of fur and claws hurtled out of the bushes, a cold stab of fear ran right through each spectator, knowing that death could come in an instant.

On the second day of the Gathering, the game went wrong.

The second day of the Gathering, Kyp chose to feed in an area the Red was known to frequent, and as usual he feigned total indifference. It was late in the second sixth, and the sun, already up for some time, had burned the dew off the grass. The air hung, still and thick and heavy. The Red first appeared in the small rectangular opening of his human's roost: a pair of pale golden eyes glinting out from behind the clear flat stone humans place over their roost openings. Moments later, his presence was felt in the dark loam and shadows beneath the raspberry canes — like a chill in the air. Then, the faintest sound of stirring leaves betrayed a gathering of coiled muscles, a shifting of paws, a tensing of sinews — the Red preparing his approach. Then the explosion — a deadly blur of hurtling fur and limbs, a crush of branches swinging forward and snapping back. Kyp sprang into the air just ahead of the claws and teeth, but this time the Red didn't fall to the earth to sprawl in a heap. This time the Red only feinted in the direction of Kyp, then continued fast, fast, *fast* across the grass. Too late, everyone became aware of a small black presence feeding on the ground, on the *other side* of the bushes. Kyp swung back, simultaneously sounding a warning.

The newling, Klea, panicked. Unable to see the Red, uncertain of what direction the danger was coming from because she was screened by the bushes, Klea sprang from the grass and, ignoring the urgent calls from above, sped into the bushes and directly into the Red as he burst through the canes. In an instant the Red pounced, pinning Klea to the dirt and clamping his powerful jaws around her back and neck. Kyp dove at the Red, trying to distract the big cat, then dove again. He shouted and taunted. Within moments, Kymmy appeared, and both dove. And though they approached closer than they should have and stayed longer than was safe, the Red simply sank deeper into the shadowy protection of the thorny raspberry canes, the tiny dark body hanging limply from his mouth.

When he finally did leave, some time after midday, he left little Klea's poor broken body in plain view on the edge of the lawn, baking in the sun. He hadn't even been hungry.

CHAPTER 7

That evening was a restless, edgy one. Some spent the long night grieving. Some were still in shock, unable to grasp their loss. Outrage mingled with pain and regret, and of course guilt as well, because everyone, on some level, realized that they had contributed to the death of that poor innocent. If someone had sounded the alarm earlier, if everyone had not had such faith in Kyp's abilities, if even *one* of us had not been so attentive to the game, little Klea would not have been caught. But we were, and so she was.

Kyp especially had been restless. Unable to sit or sleep for even a few moments, he shuttled continually through the night, flying aimlessly, returning to his perch and then repeating the cycle.

The following morning, the sun rose like an ember, edging the grass, leaves and clouds crimson. I greeted the day from atop one of those tall lights humans build near their pathways. Say what you wish about humans, there's nothing I enjoy better than wrapping my wings and body around one of those devices, feeling its warmth spreading through my belly and up into my shoulder muscles. The heat works wonders for these old bones. When my joints have been acting up, it makes me want to throw my head back and praise the Maker for making the human. In any case, that's where I was that morning, half awake, half asleep, aware only of the heat radiating through these old bones.

Kyp, as always, was one of the first to rise and feed. A slight breeze blew from the northwest, bumping and jangling the bits of stone humans hang outside their roosts. For that reason, no one heard the Red's approach.

No one suspected that the Red would return so soon. He must have been encouraged by his recent victory. I only caught sight of him as he bolted toward Kyp from under the lowest sloping branches of a tall spruce tree. Kyp lifted from the ground off balance and struck one of the wooden barriers erected by humans. He caught a glancing blow to his right wing, faltered in the air, struggled and dropped to the ground just beyond the barrier. The Red shot up and over as fast as water over a rock in a river.

Kyp tried to lift, but everyone could see that something

had gone wrong. He'd hop and flutter, fly a short space, then drop again. On his third fall, the injury must have been made worse because he was able only to run across the field in that curious limping gait he'd developed, leaping, jumping and gliding a short distance before running again. The Red, realizing that Kyp was hurt, sped up. The Call had gone out, but most of the flock were still waking, some couldn't make sense of what was happening, and many of the youngest and strongest appeared to have already gone to forage.

Kyp approached a lip in a grassy ridge, but he led the Red by only the smallest margin. The big cat coiled his muscles together and sprang full out. Kyp ducked and bounced to the left, displaying an uncanny sense of timing even with his injury. Then all at once the Red stopped.

Just beyond the lip, in a little hollow below the crest, sat thirty of the youngest, fastest, fittest crows in the Family. Without a sound, they lifted into the air. The Red had barely time to recognize the trap he'd fallen into. He twisted about and took off, but Kyp had drawn him onto a grassy expanse that offered no cover or shelter or protection: the Red was committed to a foot race over open ground, and in a race between wings and feet, bet on wings every time.

For those of you too young to have seen an organized Mob in action, it's a terrible and wonderful thing — and a thing we use only in genuine emergencies. I've seen a Mob called up to take on a fox and chase it back to its den. I've seen Mobs harass and worry lynx off their feed. I've seen them take down a mature golden eagle and then pick the carcass clean. The Red didn't have any of these experiences to draw on, but the moment he saw all those Crows silently bearing down, he raced for his life.

The Mob rose like a cloud and fell like a storm. In an instant, Crows were raking the cat's fur, pecking everywhere at once. The attack was coordinated in a way I had never witnessed before, no one bird staying close enough or long enough to get caught by the Red's flailing claws, each beak darting in to pull and poke and stab. I realized then that what I'd perceived as restlessness in Kyp the evening before had actually been him organizing this attack. By the time the Red reached the perimeter of the human enclosure, there were four, maybe five patches on his back that had been plucked bald as a crab apple. A jagged cut ran along one shoulder. This was a clear victory, and most of the Crows retreated to the Gathering Tree laughing and whooping and calling to one another. One Crow, however, refused to leave — Kuper.

Kyp urged him off, but Kuper clung to the cat like a burr. I may have mentioned that Kuper is strong — well, he set his talons to that pelt, strained his wings and actually lifted the Red's rump clean off the ground. The big cat howled and twisted, and suddenly Kuper's head darted forward and — snip, snap — his beak closed around the tip of the Red's tail. A yowl rose from the cat that put all the previous cries to shame. There in Kuper's beak was the brown and red furry tip of the tail — the Red was left waving the stump. The Red twisted and hooked his two front paws along Kuper's underbody. With a sudden yank, he dragged Kuper to the ground. They tumbled over and over, fur and feathers flying. Things might have been very bad for Kuper had Kyp not dropped onto the Red's arched neck and, with a slashing motion of his beak, opened up a cut over the Red's left eye. Distracted, the Red wheeled on Kyp, who nimbly skipped out of reach.

At that moment, the cat's master, a chunky, squat, hairy human, thundered out on the lawn waving its limbs. With a push of his wings, Kuper was out of reach and safely in the air. And there was the Red looking foolish and mad, half bald, half bloodied, that stump of a tail lashing left and right, and that one eye closed shut. The human gathered up the Red in one massive limb and backed into its roost, still shouting and shooing at Kuper with the other massive limb. What a spectacle.

But it didn't end there. Nowhere near.

CHAPTER 8

More than anything else, night is a time of second thoughts. In the dark, as one listens to crickets call and the wind gnaw on dead leaves, one has time to reflect on mistakes. Perched on a branch, in the double shade of night and shadow, one has time to brood and to wish that things were otherwise. But with the rising of the sun and the bright light of dawn, everything is revealed.

That following morning, the sun crept over the horizon. The air was still and warm and unusually heavy for the season. It felt more like summer than spring. Off to one side of the Gathering Tree, a knot of Crows conferred. Before everyone could rise and go about their errands, Kyrk emerged from that knot.

Against a pale, scorched-looking sky, he hopped to the gnarled end of a prominent branch where he knew he would draw the most attention. His one good eye roamed the tree. "I charge," he rumbled in his most penetrating voice, "Kyp ru Kurea with Reckless Mobbing. I charge him with Bringing Danger to the Flock. I ask that the Family be gathered and judgment served."

Bringing Danger to the Flock is as serious a charge as can be laid, and those perched in the tree grew quiet. Adults shushed newlings, like a small, separate wind blowing through the branches. Those in flight sensed something important and came to rest on the nearest branch. Kyrk performed a brief and fastidious preening as he waited for them to settle.

Having captured the Family's attention, he glanced about. Caught in the sun's emerging rays, each jet black feather glittered. My own plumage seemed drab by comparison, and I noted that for some reason my tail feathers had commenced shedding. Perhaps it was the weather, perhaps it was the stress of the migration, but for whatever reason, some feathers were only barely clinging to my tail, and more than a few were lying forlornly on the ground. I felt inadequate stepping out on the limb with my shaggy, raggedy tail, but as Chooser, I am compelled to preside over any formal gathering or declaration, so up I stepped.

Had correct procedure been followed, Kyrk would have first consulted me, but Kyrk has never felt any pressing need to consult anyone, so I had neither warning nor time for preparation. I took my position on a branch to the north and east side of the tree, tucked my wings back and waited to see how things would unfold.

"You ask for judgment and the Kinaar is listening," I called, delivering the formal reply. "If you have a case, you must state it. If the Family finds in your favor, we must enforce it."

He acknowledged me with only the slightest nod. "Two days ago, Kyp ru Kurea," he began, again giving Kyp his formal Clan name, "knowingly attracted the Red's attention. He baited, taunted and drew him out. The result? One newling dead."

A voice from somewhere farther down the tree called, "Not the first time a cat has caught newlings."

"Let him finish," I murmured.

"Absolutely." Kyrk nodded his head. "But if a newling dies because the Rule of Three is broken, then there's responsibility to be considered."

That hushed everyone. The Rule of Three is one of our most basic directives. When three or more go out together, one keeps watch. We're cautioned about this over and over from the time we remove the shell. Without due attention to the primary rules of order and responsibility, the flock could never survive — it wouldn't *be* a flock, because what is a flock but individuals who have agreed to abide by a set of rules? If Kyp had put someone at risk because of his failure to perform backup, it would be hard — very hard — for the flock to forgive.

"In addition," Kyrk continued, "Kyp organized and directed a Mob during a Gathering. This Mob was enjoined without proper consultation —"

"Are you siding with the cat?" a sour voice hissed. It was Koren, one of Kyp's young friends who, I was fairly certain, had participated in the Mobbing.

"Let him speak," I repeated.

"*No*, I'm not siding with the cat," Kyrk responded, fixing his good eye on Koren, "and you'd know if you were old enough to recall that I've been involved in a number of authorized Mobbings. But never one like this. Never one that knowingly attracted the *attention of humans*."

Several loud murmurs of "That's right" emerged from the knot that Kyrk had been in, but they were echoed right through the tree.

"Nor one that put the Gathering Tree at risk. Consider this!" he said, raising his voice slightly and turning to include more of the flock. "If we were to Mob every cat that hunted a Crow, where would it end? Wouldn't it set us against every *human* master as well? How long would humans tolerate us? *If* this particular human is angry enough, *if* this particular human is upset enough, *if* this particular human calls on other humans because we're harassing his slaves — then what? Who can stand against the human? This Mob action was irresponsible, undisciplined and — worst of all — unnecessary."

By now there were murmurs coming from up and down the tree, and Kyp's friends had grown curiously quiet. Kyrk was set to go on, but I had to stop him for a moment. "I want to be clear here. You have three charges you wish to pursue, then? The first is Reckless Mobbing during a Gathering. The second is that Kyp broke the Rule of Three. And the third, and most serious, that Kyp Brought Danger to the Flock. Are you saying that the danger came about as a result of his altercation with the Red or as a result of the Mobbing?"

"Both. Had he not taunted the Red, none of this would have happened. Had he any thought for the welfare of his Family, he would not have raised a Mob without proper consultation."

"Very well. You have all heard Kyrk's charges. This is a Family matter, and we of the Kinaar make decisions about the Family as a Family. If you wish to bear witness or dispute testimony, that is your right and duty, and now is the time. Take your place on the branch and be seen by the Family."

"I have a statement to make." A small voice emerged from the middle of the tree, and Kymmy fluttered up onto the branch next to me. "I have to clarify something. The Rule of Three can't apply in this case because there were only two on the ground. Kyp and Klea."

"You were seen flying *up* to assist Klea," Kyrk said sternly. "Therefore you *must* have been on the ground with them. You know the rules, Kym. When three or more go out, they go as a team, and one must perform lookout. It seems plain to me that the only way Kyp could avoid this charge is if someone else was performing backup. I had assumed it was his responsibility; he's the eldest of you three. Are you telling me it was *yours*?"

"Excuse me, perhaps I'm not being clear." Kym bobbed her head and cleared her throat at the same time. Kyrk was exerting all his considerable influence and pressure on her. Combined with a steady stare, his feathers were gradually rising round his neck and shoulders, increasing his size by almost half and making him a most intimidating presence.

"No, you're not," he replied sternly.

"I'm sorry, sir. But, technically, I wasn't *on* the ground. I was *close* to the ground. I'm not trying to excuse myself, I mean, it was careless on my part too. I should have communicated with the others, but I was actually in the raspberry canes, just a bit above the ground. So … I don't think the Rule of Three —"

"Nonsense. That doesn't make a peck of difference," Kyrk interrupted brusquely. "If you were engaged in the *same* activity as the others and in the same vicinity, on ground or slightly above ground doesn't matter."

"Yes, well, exactly."

"Exactly *what*? Were you foraging with them or not?"

"No. I *wasn't*. That's what I'm saying."

Kyrk stopped. "You weren't?"

"No, sir."

"Well, then …," he sputtered. "Well." He turned his attention to me. "Well, this is obviously a case of a friend offering protection," he snorted and looked back at Kym. "What else would you have been doing? What else *could* you have been doing?"

Kym sat silently.

"You must answer his question," I reminded her.

"Yes, of course." She cleared her throat. "Human watching, actually, sir."

From the involuntary snap of his head, I could tell that this caught Kyrk off guard every bit as much as it did me. "Human watching?"

"Yes, sir. Through the little clear openings in their roosts."

"For what possible reason?"

"Because, I find them …" Kym's voice trailed away.

"Speak up," Kyrk snapped.

"I find them interesting."

"You find them interesting?"

"Yes, sir. I was positioned in the bushes low down, looking up in the opposite direction, at the humans who were crouched and eating inside their dwelling. Which is why I never saw Klea, or Kyp, or the Red for that matter. And, please, I don't know that you could call me Kyp's friend. I barely know him."

"Well. Well, if you weren't in communication, you *should* have been," Kyrk fumed, frustrated that his case had been weakened in front of the Family. "That's very careless. *Very* careless. You should always remain in communication when others are nearby. Even if you are *human* watching. This doesn't do you much credit, does it?"

"No, sir, it doesn't. But it's the truth."

"Thank you, Kymmy," I said, feeling sorry for her as she fluttered back to her perch. "Do you have anything further you wish to say, Kyrk?"

"Yes. This ... statement — this *suspicious* statement — doesn't alter the *effect* of Kyp's activities. Nor does it alter in any way the remaining two charges. That Kyp raised a Mob without consultation during a Gathering and that he placed the entire Family at risk. Some of you may find some sense of accomplishment in seeing the Red chased back to its human. Some of you seem to have found it comical. I say there was neither humor nor glory in yesterday's deeds. Kyp's misguided actions only *increased* a risk that already exists. The Gathering Tree stands just a short distance from the human. Tell me this, everyone who enjoyed a laugh yesterday — when the human returns to chase us, how many of you will be laughing? That's all I have to say."

I squinted around through the rustling leaves. There was lots of whispered conversation, but it was impossible to tell if there was any consensus.

"Consulting," croaked Keir, one of the more venerable members of the Koorda Clan, as he struggled up to perch beside me. The branch quivered as he landed, and he hung on desperately while it steadied and he regained his balance. I was surprised to see him make an appearance before the Family. He's my age, but over the past few years has grown increasingly frail. I had half expected him not to make the Gathering this year, so I was doubly surprised to see him taking part in this. He himself looked surprised, blinking several times and squinting suspiciously down at the perch as though it might start moving once more.

"I, ahm, just want to be clear about that, ahm, that *word*. It seems to me, that is, if I recollect correctly, there must have been thirty or so individuals in the Mobbing, although I didn't count, so I can't say for sure." He stopped and blinked again. "There *must* certainly have been more than twenty because I recall noticing *ten* or *eleven* on the Red at one time, and there were at least twice that number in the air."

"Probably thirty or so," I agreed, hoping to move Keir along in his testimony.

"Quite so. At least thirty."

"What is your point?" Kyrk asked. "The law says that during a Gathering the entire Family must be consulted unless an emergency exists. There was no emergency. There was no consultation of the entire Family. Therefore it's plain —"

"I'm sorry," Keir gently interrupted. "Excuse me. The law *says* 'the Family,' not 'the entire Family.' The implication, that is, the true *sense* of that, ahm, *particular* phrasing may *be* that the *entire* Family be consulted, but that is not, in fact, the way it is worded. And if the matter that we are considering now is whether or not there was consultation, well, it seems to me there *must* have been some consultation. Maybe not formally. Perhaps not with the elders. Certainly not with me. But unless one can perform a Mob on one's own — and I don't see how one can — unless one can, ahm, *separate* oneself into many different selves and so become a Mob all by oneself, then it seems to me there must have been *some* consultation, don't you think? Or how else did those, ahm, *several* individuals arrive at the *same* place at the *same* time?"

"Yes, yes," Kyrk barked. "There was *planning*. I'm not saying there wasn't *planning*. But that is not the same as *consultation*. Consultation of the Family is something more extensive than that —"

"Is it?" Keir asked, peering over his beak at Kyrk. "Is it indeed, Kyrk ru Kurea? Perhaps so, but that's not clear. But perhaps it's not the *absence* of consultation that you object to so much as who was and who was *not* consulted."

Keir concluded as gently as he had begun, then limped off the branch and glided to a lower perch.

"Does anyone else wish to speak to this matter?" I asked. Somewhere, down near the base of the tree, a newling whispered, "I'm hungry. I wanna go hunting." His mother quickly shushed him as Ketch, a big shaggy easterner, fluttered up to the branch next to me and puffed out his breast. Ketch has always had a habit of stabbing his beak as he talked, of *jabbing* with each *word* for *emphasis* in a way that's always reminded me of a woodpecker, and he started his testimony with just such a quick thrust.

"The *Maker*," he said, "is laughing at us. The Maker knows the rules. *She* made the rules, and when we break those rules, or ignore those rules, we spit in her eye. Klea was from our Clan, the Kemna. I knew her and watched over her from the time she was perched out on a bowl of twigs at the end of a branch. And I want to say I couldn't agree more with what Kyrk is saying. I *couldn't. Agree. More,*" poking vigorously with each word. "*Who* does this Kyp think he is? The law? *Above* the law? Well, I just want to tell him — and tell all of you — *no one* is above the law. The law is the law and no one is above it. The Maker said to Crows back in First Times, 'Here is the law. You live by it always.'"

Ketch took a deep breath as if to continue, then realized he had nothing new to add. In a rush of exhaled air, he concluded. "Anyway, that's what I believe and no one's going to convince me otherwise, and let me tell you one other thing about the law — no silly, jack-jawing, fresh-out-of-the-nest Crow can bend it, twist it or break it. Not even if they can perform all the tricks and air acrobatics in the world. The law is the law, and if you love the Maker you'll obey it, and that's all I have to say."

He hopped off the branch, and as he did so, I saw Keta drop away from the tree and then slowly spiral up and back. Keta's only a few years younger than me, but is as respected a Crow as there is. She's one of the few remaining members of her nest-family to survive and recollect the murderous blizzard that swept the great plains two decades back, and she's still sharp as a falcon's talon. Her legs aren't what they used to be, so she took her own good time to choose an open perch and landed soft as thistledown.

"The law is the law," she repeated, blinking solemnly, then slowly let her gaze sweep the tree. Now, I happen to know that Keta's eyesight is little better than poor, so there is no possible way she could have seen Ketch or anyone else at any distance, but it looked as if she was peering deeply into the eyes of each and every Crow perched in that tree.

"Well," she said, finally, "maybe the law is the law, but the Maker, as I understand her, isn't roosting with us tonight, so you all will have to excuse me if I ask for someone with bigger wings than Ketch here to speak for her. It seems to me that there's always someone, somewhere, trying to misuse the law and knock someone over the head with it, when I've always been of the understanding that the law was constructed to uplift and guide and support us. This instance today seems to me like a very good example of 'head bashing.' Little Klea is dead, and that's a tragic thing to happen to a youngster just finding her way in the world. I feel terrible for the Family. I feel terrible for her Clan as well and feel the loss personally. I didn't know her well, but she seemed to be a sweet and gentle and kind little chick. When something like this happens, when an innocent gets ripped from this world and her loved ones, I can't help but feel hurt and angry. I'm sure we all do.

"Kyp here makes an excellent target for that anger. After all, he's young. He's arrogant in that insufferable way young Crows can be. He's got the irritating habit of not listening at the precise moment that he ought to. But I don't think anyone here would argue that he is a bad Crow, or an evil Crow; and in our hearts, we know that sometimes bad things happen, and even good Crows can get caught. There's no doubt that Kyp acted recklessly and should be admonished for that recklessness, but *should* he be punished for circumstances that, if we're honest, we must admit were not entirely of his own making?

"Kym has already come forward, in a very responsible manner, to point out that the Rule of Three was *not* broken. Still, Ketch and Kyrk here insist that there's a responsibility to be settled, and I say fair enough. But you listen to me, all of you. Make sure you sort things out right, because there's *plenty* of responsibility to go round. I say shame on Kyp for letting a dangerous game spin out of control. And shame on him for taking it upon himself to fix things without consulting the Family. That's not the way we do things, that's not a *Crow's* way.

"But after you're good and done with Kyp, tell me this — *who was* looking after little Klea? What, for goodness sake, was she doing on the ground, in broad daylight, unescorted and unsupervised? We Crows have a responsibility to raise our young. We're not *cowbirds* that push their chicks out of the nest and forget about them. I want to know what in the world that young one was doing on the ground unwatched when everyone knows the Red is as bad a cat as ever was.

"The Maker admonishes us to help one another and to raise our young to be good members of the flock, but there are some at this Gathering who should be taking responsibility and aren't. Where was her Clan? Why hadn't *she* made contact with Kyp? We all know that when a group moves, they stay in contact — well, what was she thinking? As my great-aunt used to say, 'There's more to raising a chick than stealing an egg,' and I certainly don't need anyone who can't even look after their offspring and kin to lecture *me* on the Maker. This law, *our* law, is meant to help us make decisions and raise and instruct our young Crows. It is one of our finest creations, something that separates us from your magpies and jays and the other lesser creatures. Don't let it be misused to exact punishment or revenge. And that's all *I* have to say."

She barely had time to leave the perch when Kork, a stringy elder with a long lean neck, nearly bounced off his perch. "You all know me. I'm senior in the Kemna Clan and I want to say we don't *need* any advice about how to raise our chicks, thank you very much. Our Clan has been hatching chicks for many a generation now, and there's some who should keep their beaks shut and look after the mess in their own nest. This is about Kyp and his lawbreaking and his misdoings. In our Clan, we put our faith in the Maker and take care of ourselves.

"And another thing. Seems like I'm hearing a lot of yammering — here and elsewhere — about egg eating. I want to tell you, I eat eggs. I eat them when I find them, and all my nest-family do, too, and there's *nothing* that's going to stop us. *All* living things are made to be eaten one way or another, and I don't see that eggs are any different from the living things we find on the tree or the dead things we find on the ground." He peered belligerently up into the tree. "And if anyone has any complaint, then they should say so straight up and not make references to it where it doesn't belong, and that's all I have to say on that matter."

Now these seemingly unrelated remarks were in response to a dispute that has been simmering in the Family for I don't know how long about whether it is proper to raid the nests of other birds. And it had blown up during the migration through the mountains, after Kork and a few others had savaged a robin's nest. Keta had declared then that if the Kemnas were going to bring further dishonor on the Family with their egg-eating ways, maybe it would be better if they left the Family and instead joined a magpie reunion. I myself have no particular position on the egg-eating matter and I certainly didn't want to reopen that debate. I was all set to shut down any further discussion and move directly to the judgment when Kerda fluttered up and took her place on the perch, and all talking stopped dead. Kerda was, of course, Klea's mother.

CHAPTER 9

Kerda perched still as a stone for a long moment before speaking. When finally she began, her beak barely opened. "There's been a lot of talk," she started quietly, then abruptly stopped. I saw her breathe deeply as she seemingly studied the sky and the trees. Then she began again. "A lot of talk. Both last night, and now. Today. Everyone has been talking, and I guess I have something to say, too. The Red stole my chick, my youngest, my soul. I'd rather have died a hundred times than have seen my little Klea fly to the Maker before me. But there's nothing I can do about it. She's gone and flown. I can't tell you how I feel because there aren't words enough for it." And again she stopped. And sat. And all the Family sat with her, still and attentive. I thought the poor thing had finished but hadn't the strength to leave the branch. Then, as suddenly as she'd stopped, she began speaking again, even more quietly than before.

"I may have been a good or bad mother. I've been trying to figure out which all night, running it through my mind. To tell you the truth, I haven't decided. But I can tell you *one thing*. That Mob action may have been unwanted by Kyrk, but *I* wanted it. I wanted it and more. I've got no complaint with it except that that cat — that cat is *still* alive, still roaming the raspberry canes and hunting birds, and my baby's dead and nothing but feathers in the wind now. And who will put a judgment on the Red for my grief and my loss and my poor, cold chick?"

And with that, Kerda spread her wings and quietly glided to another thicket of aspen. I saw a couple of others glide after her to provide support and keep her company. There was more talking after that, but nothing of any substance. I could see Kyrk and his bunch trying to keep the crowd stirred up, but most had lost heart. I decided to put the question out.

"What punishment do you suggest?" I asked.

Kyrk spoke one word. "Banishment."

Throughout the tree, one could hear clucking and fussing. Banishment is as serious a punishment as we have, and I could tell from the noise running through the Flock that most couldn't support it. But I also could tell that the Flock was dangerously split on the issue. I hopped farther out on the branch, felt it sway under my feet with each hop.

"Kyrk has summoned judgment from the Family, and the judgment he asks for is Banishment. How shall we make the judgment, by Call or by Choice?"

By Call would have meant that the entire Family was compelled to express their opinion, one by one. It's a fair process, but it can take an entire day or two and is saved for only the most critical decisions. By Choice means the decision is left to the Chooser. To me.

A silence fell over the Family. I waited a long moment and then said, "Very well. By Choice."

"Kyrk has called for Banishment. Banishment means an individual is outcast, required to leave the Family and never return. He or she can have no further dealings or contact with the Family on pain of being Mobbed. They are dead to the Family forever. Their name is stricken from our records. It cannot be spoken or used again for three generations. This judgment is reserved for the most extreme crimes. Murder. Raiding Family nests. Crimes that involve willful ill intent. I say Banishment is, in this instance, inappropriate. This was recklessness, not ill intent.

"The Family has elected for the Choice, and there are three judgments in my Choice. First, I say that foraging in the area nearest human dwellings shall cease for the

69

duration of the Gathering, as will pestering of their cats and so forth. Kyrk was entirely correct in making this point. We cannot afford to provoke the human.

"Second, I want to say there can be no Mobbing without consultation of the Family while a Gathering is in effect, unless it is to react to an emergency. If a hawk appears overhead, yes, by all means, don't hesitate to put out the Call. But don't arrange something for the next day without consulting first. That's only common sense, and, Kyp, that's where you should have done things differently.

"Finally, there is the third judgment, concerning Bringing Danger to the Flock. Has Kyp, in fact, brought the Family into danger? The arrangement between Crow and human has always been a delicate one. With the human comes a bounty of food, but who can tell when the human will get angry? As the saying goes, 'Three things can't be foretold: The path of the storm, the moment of a hatching and the temper of the human.' I've seen humans come with stingers and kill good Crows for no reason whatsoever. Other times they seem friendly and gentle. Who knows what the human is thinking and what will provoke them? Still it can't be good to bring the human out to protect its cat, especially when we're in the middle of a Gathering. Kyp, can you come to this perch?"

Kyp flew up and sat, stiff and silent. I looked hard at him.

You know, it's in moments like those that you actually *see* someone, and for the first time I truly *saw* Kyp. Jet black eyes. Bony under the feathers, scrawny in the leg, not as fine a coat as he might have, even a little scruffy — but that's not a bad thing necessarily. The shiniest coats cover the sort of Crow who is always preening. I realized though that the stiffness and awkwardness were slowly disappearing, and Kyp was growing up. He'd never be one of our larger Crows, but a Crow is more than what he seems on the outside, and looking at him I could see some intelligence, some ignorance, but, more than anything else, *desire*. Desire, in this case, to do better than he'd done in the past.

"Kyp," I asked, "have you anything to say before I set final judgment?"

"No." His eyes roved until he found Kerda, who had returned to hear the judgment. "I'm truly sorry for the part I played in Klea's death. I'd do anything to have that moment back. I wanted to help her, I really did, but I was too late." He stopped and, for a long silent moment, he and Kerda locked eyes. Who knows what thoughts passed between those two? Then Kyp dipped his head. "I accept the judgment."

I cleared my throat. "Our traditions say six is a sacred number. Six is the number of the cardinal directions. North, south, east, west, up and down. Six is the number of days the Maker sat on the sacred first nest. Great Crow first

Chapter 10

I'd no sooner pronounced his verdict when I was flooded by memories of Kyp. I recollected the spring he hatched. All the eggs of that nesting came out thin. Kyp's egg cracked early, and he crawled from the shell featherless, wet and barely breathing. As often as he tried to stand, he'd fall over, and it was soon apparent one leg was shorter than the other. I'm not sure he would have survived if he'd shared the nest, but his was the only egg to hatch. His mother spent all her energy keeping young Kyp alive, and even at that he was late to fledge and then late to fly.

Once he started flying, though — Great Crow! — I have never seen a bird take to air so readily. By the time the Family gathered for fall migration, Kyp was still a runt, but there was no doubt he would survive the trip. His landings were crude. His forage time spent on the ground was a trial, but he was already more able in the air than almost anyone else in the flock. That was the season Kyrk saw all of his grandchicks perish — he called it the Bad Luck brood — and I think he held it against Kyp that he returned south with us that fall. Well, I thought, Kyrk has finally paid him back.

Now, Eviction doesn't approach the severity of Banishment by a long stretch. Six days is long enough to get hungry and lonely, but every Crow in his lifetime will spend considerably more time than that out on his own. But to be separated from the Flock during a Gathering, to be separated until the Gathering is almost done — that's both hard and shameful. It meant much more than just missing out on the social aspects of the Gathering for one Kyp's age. It meant missing out on one of very few opportunities to find a suitable mate. There were plenty of eligible females at the Gathering, almost all being courted by someone. Eviction meant you might miss your *one* occasion to nest up, and if the next season proved unfavorable, if you were injured or for some reason could not make it to the Gathering, it might mean never having nestlings of your own. As well, if the rest of the Flock decided that you weren't nesting material — and the shame of an Eviction might be sufficient to do just that — it might mean feeling compelled to leave and join another Flock.

Now, an important thing happened just before Kyp flew off, a thing unseen and unheard by most because I was still finishing my pronouncement. Kuper, on a branch just below Kyp, whispered to him, "Follow the river west until you come to the fork. Take the southerly branch as far as it goes. There's good feeding and safe roosting to be found there."

Kyp looked down at Kuper, but Kuper had turned to preen the feathers of his right leg. I had, by this time, finished my pronouncement and the flock was silent. Kyp scanned the faces of his Family, then lifted his wings and flew.

It is one thing to be on your own and an entirely different thing to be *sent* out alone. When one is Evicted, a cold, hollow feeling settles beneath your breastbone, like a chigger under the skin. It aches, nags and gnaws at you, and it won't let you be.

Kyp drifted off, directionless as a milkweed seed carried by the wind. The Family watched him trail away until he became a dark speck against the sky, and then nothing at all.

Who knows what his thoughts were as he flew off? Who can tell what secret regrets he had in the privacy of his own reflections? Who can say what he would have done differently? Everyone has these thoughts confined in the deep recesses of one's own soul.

Kym approached me on my branch. "Uncle," she said quietly, "you know the judgment isn't right."

I continued looking off in the direction Kyp had flown. "It's as right as I could make it. Kyp shouldn't have angered those old ones. It was a near enough thing not getting him Banished. Now, I'm tired. I'm going to take a long ant bath and try to forget some of the things that were said this morning."

CHAPTER 11

I'm of several minds about Eviction. Of course it's never pleasant, and it can be dangerous. A Crow on his own can run into the kind of trouble that only many Crows can manage. Still, Eviction is simply the way the Family tells someone "You have some thinking to do, on your own," and I'm of the view that thinking, in and of itself, can never be a bad thing. You can never suffer from too much thinking.

If Kyp seemed directionless initially it was because he *was* directionless. For a few moments, a wave of self-pity rolled over him. Evicted. Humiliated. Every wrong decision, every error he had ever made returned to him during that long, lone flight. Then he decided upon a course of action.

Anyone who tells you they have nothing they're ashamed of is either the newest newling or a fool. Everyone makes mistakes. It's what one does *after* one has made his or her biggest mistakes that takes the full measure of a Crow. Kyp decided to follow Kuper's advice. He caught a down draft into the valley, then maneuvered along the banks of the river. It's always possible to find a stronger, faster draft just above the main current, in the middle, but there you're out in the open for all your eagles and ospreys to view.

I've said this before, too — efficient flying isn't so much about brawn as it is about brain. Why is it that some of us elders come into roost at the end of a day of migrating and have more energy and wing left in reserve than some of the newlings? It's reading the winds. It's selecting the right breeze. It's judging which will carry you longest in the direction you're going. Listen to me, all you young ones, learn to interpret the wind and you will find yourself moving in a gentle, easy rhythm with nature. Fail to learn that skill and you'll wear yourself to the quill before you reach maturing.

In any case, I was talking about Kyp and what he was doing and all. Kyp caught a draft that took him downstream. When he came to a fork, he turned south. The branch grew narrower, and signs of humans diminished. The trees along the riverbanks grew older and taller, with many projecting out over the water. The current ran slower, the river bottom dropped, and the water's surface became still and calm and a deep, rich gray green. On Kyp flew, and the river grew narrower still.

There were by now no signs of human roosts or human feeding. The wind had dropped and the air was still. Kyp slipped between the trees cautiously. Abruptly the valley opened up.

A beaver dam had been thrown up across the stream, flooding parts of the forest. The valley's walls drew up around this little lake, snug and tight. The glade and lake created a neat, compact haven ringed by tall tree cover and the steep cliff abutments. Birds of all sorts nestled in the branches and trunks of the teetering waterlogged trees: kingfishers, woodpeckers, swifts and swallows. In the water and by the lake's edges were loons, grebes and geese. Along the south shore, an immense and ancient willow sprawled and swayed. In all ways, it was as beautiful and calm as the first river that ran through the first valley at the beginning of all time.

Kyp circled the gorge to scout it out, then dropped to a thin springy branch on a bushy alder. He felt a soft gust of wind and turned his head just as Kuper landed on the branch next to him.

"You took your time getting here," the big Crow said as he stretched his neck to work out a knot.

Kyp stared at Kuper. "What are you doing here?"

Kuper ducked his head under a wing to rearrange one of his secondary feathers. "Thought you might need company."

"But — but, you can't be seen with me."

Kuper glanced about at the empty valley. "So, who's watching?"

"Don't you understand? If someone catches you, you'll be up for judgment as well."

"Like I said, who's here besides you and me? Relax." Kuper drawled and spread his wings to catch some sun. "Before I joined the Family, I flew solo. I followed the migrations and shadowed the Gathering, stayed to myself and watched all of you from a distance. Some nights I'd slip off here for a quiet roost and no one ever ventured this way. Anyway, I'm not afraid of being forced out on my own, if it comes to that. I've spent most of my life on my own. So," he said, changing the subject, "was I right about this place?"

"It's beautiful," Kyp allowed, realizing Kuper wasn't about to leave. "And humans never come here?"

"Oh, well, you know humans. They *own* the earth, don't they? They're everywhere. But they don't live here, and only occasionally *walk* here. On their own or in twos or threes. Like ghosts, they appear early in the first sixth or later in the final sixth, just before dark. But they never roost here."

"Why?"

"Old Kalum says it best: 'Who knows why humans do

what they do?' Maybe it's taboo for them to come at certain times, maybe it's forbidden. Maybe they're just lazy. But I like to think that it's just too nice a place for humans. They have to have their stone paths, smoke and noise, and ugly moving boxes. This sort of place, the way the Maker made it — maybe it just doesn't interest them."

Kyp scanned the sky. "How come none of the Family comes here?"

"Too far from the Gathering Tree and the humans' giant cache. Why would any Crow in his right mind roam as far as *this* for something to eat," Kuper asked sardonically, "when the humans have laid out a feast a short hop away? Speaking of food — you hungry?"

For the first time since the judgment, Kyp felt a pang in his belly and realized he'd had nothing all day. "I could eat."

"There's a place over by the cliff's edge. Plenty of tadpoles and water sliders to be had. Have you tasted those small water beetles?"

"The green ones?"

"Yeah." Kuper cocked his head as the image flashed in his mind. "Aren't they *good?*"

"You can find those here?"

"Only along the south shoreline. But plenty of them. Come on. I'll show you."

I have to add that, personally, I *love* water beetles. As a younger Crow, I used to consider them the perfect end to any meal. I regard them as a gift from the Maker to our taste buds. Crunchy on the outside, juicy on the inside, zesty. I could sit on a rock at the beginning of spring and do nothing but sift through reeds, getting my fill. Some say meat, salvaged or fresh, is a Crow's most important meal, and I enjoy meat as much as any, but I believe in balance — a little meat, a little fruit, some greens and a healthy supply of bugs. Bugs put a sheen on your feathers like nothing else. In fact, if I didn't believe in balance as heartily as I do, I could live on bugs and berries alone. Those tiny green shiny-backed beetles in the spring and the great, fat, sassy red-winged hoppers in the fall, and for dessert *blackberries* ready to drop from the branch. Your strawberries are nice enough, and I love a good grouseberry — although they're so puny it's hard to get even a beakful unless you're prepared to hunt and peck a bit. But blackberries — oh my — they're not only delicious, they're beautiful to look at — each dark berry separated into tiny, fine, fat shimmering globes of juice. One bite and a burst of nectar pours down the throat. And the wonderful thing is that in any given bush, there's sufficient to satisfy even a generous appetite. But don't get me started on bugs or berries.

So, where was I? Oh yes, I was telling you about Kyp and Kuper leaving that tree. There you have them — two Crows who shouldn't have been together, leaping from the branch and gliding down through the trees … and barely escaping with their lives. They'd only just left the branch when a soft whoosh was heard — very quiet, like nature drawing a quick breath — and then a thump. Kuper was knocked from behind, tumbling head over tail feathers through the air.

CHAPTER 12

Kyp and Kuper had made the cardinal error — careless inspection before leaving the perch. A scattering of feathers fell from the sky, and Kyp feared that Kuper had been knocked to the earth. And he *would* have been, had he not heard that soft rush of air and intuitively moved to the right. He *would* have become a meal for the owl that had slipped from its roost in a hoary old cottonwood and been following them, silent as death. It had chosen its spot carefully, dropping like a dead weight on Kuper's unprotected back, and had only missed sinking its outstretched talons into him because of Kuper's canny shift. This wasn't just any owl, either. This was a mature Great Horned. A Crow eater.

Kyp immediately did what we're all trained to do, he slipped in beside the owl and called loudly, both to distract it and to attract the attention of any help in the area. As you know, an owl, even a big owl, can be chased off with a concerted effort of say seven or eight adult crows. And a bigger Mob has been known to kill them on occasion, so the Owl Family knows not to fool with us when the numbers are on our side. But no one replied. On this day, there were only the two of them to deal with this hungry owl.

Kuper chose this particular moment to do something unheard of. All Crows know — we're taught from the time we're an egg — that when the horned owl appears, you lose it in the bushes. They're good fliers and strong fliers, your owls, but their size and weight become a disadvantage down among the scrub. We have this repeated to us time and time again, until it becomes second nature: "If an owl does hover, first fly for cover." Instead, Kuper rolled once, came up behind that owl, stooped and attacked.

Now, a Great Horned isn't as big as your golden eagle, and it's not as fast as your osprey or your falcon. But when it comes to Crow killing, there's no bird like it. They've got weight on their side, they've got size and strength, and they're skillful, silent fliers. They can ride the air, flutter, stall and maneuver — they look big but fly small and quick and mean. No right-thinking Crow will ever engage a Great Horned in an air duel — but that's exactly what Kuper did.

He took the owl on its tail, and he raked it over its hindquarters, clawing and pecking.

Now, in my time, I've seen Crows come and go, but I can't bring to mind a Crow with the same size and wingspan as Kuper. I've even heard it rumored that there was some raven in him. But this time he had picked a battle he simply could not win. One on one, I have never seen a Crow best an owl, and frankly I don't ever expect to.

Well, when Kuper landed on the posterior of that owl, I'm not sure who was more surprised, Kyp or the Great Horned. Kyp must have thought Kuper had lost his mind. He rallied, put out another call for help and then did what any Crow would have done — he flew in close to the nape of the owl's thick neck. Of course the Great Horned, like all devil birds of its kind, can rotate his head nearly around completely — so this owl was flying and staring back at the crazy Crow pecking at its behind and studying just how exactly he was going to kill him. He took Kuper by the right leg with his sharp hooked beak and gave it a good shake, so he wasn't expecting anything from Kyp. But Kyp chose his moment, stretched his neck out, plucked a beakful of feathers from the owl's mantle and flew off.

Now the Great Horned started to lose his temper. He'd had enough fooling around. He cranked his big fat owl head around, focused that deadly orange gaze square on Kyp and veered off in his direction. Of course, Kyp knew this would happen. He had intended for it to happen. Newlings, *listen* — listen and learn. That's all part of evasive maneuvers. Kyp had provided Kuper with a classic distraction, and this was Kuper's cue to make his escape as Kyp also took to the brush. Instead, Kuper let out a loud, hoarse cry and pounced on the great bird's back, pecking and clawing and riding it like a chick playing Bounce on a wind-tossed branch. And in doing that, he did something he never should have done — he put that big brown and gray owl into a fury.

The Great Horned stalled, let out a bark like a dog and turned over. He shrugged Kuper off his massive shoulders like so much dust, and with a great wide flap of his enormous gray wings curled round and came back at Kuper, claws out, big yellow eyes and enormous sharp beak wide open. And that would have been the end of Kuper — snip snap, and nothing left but feathers and a bit of scattered bones and owl pellets in the dirt later on — had Kyp not pulled a tight circle as well and, using the whip force of that turn, driven up underneath into the owl's soft belly. For a moment, he knocked the wind out of the owl, disorienting it. This was, after all, the last thing the owl expected. Here he was preparing to dine on Crow and instead he feels this stabbing pain, and this insignificant Crow he thinks he has already chased off is underneath him again.

If that big owl had connected, big and angry as he was,

Kuper would have become an owl snack. Instead, things were as bad as they possibly could get for Kyp. See, the one place you do not, under any circumstances, want to be found is *beneath* the grasping talons of a Great Horned owl. An owl of that size doesn't have to hit you with speed, although most often it will. It doesn't have to snap your neck with its beak, although sometimes it does. It can kill you simply by drawing in those immense claws — they're that strong and sharp.

Now, Kyp found himself beneath the belly of an owl who could maneuver, who had weight on its side and whose talons were only a feather's breadth from his neck. Kuper had to act fast to save his friend. He leaped on that owl, sat hard on his shoulders and pecked and stabbed for all he was worth. But an owl's thick head is built to withstand abuse. It's padded by feather and bone, and that Great Horned was in a killing rage. All he could see was Kyp below. He stretched those big shaggy talons and *squeezed.*

It's then that Kyp did something I'd never heard of, and I've been around for long enough to hear nearly everything. He rolled and flew on his back — difficult enough. You all know you've got to have a master's control to fly any distance upside down, and you've got to have the right wind on your side. Wrong wind and you'll drop like a rock. So there he was, flying upside down, level and controlled — and he took the fight to the owl, like that — *upside down.*

Clawing, and stabbing with his beak just as he would ordinarily have done, blocking those great furry owl talons and parrying them with his own — only every movement he made he had to compensate for being upside down, and the slightest wrong twitch or flutter and he'd fall, and then that owl would come down on him like mites on a magpie.

Well, I'd never heard of it, and I don't believe that owl could have either. Suddenly caught between one crazy Crow above and another even crazier below, facing Crow talons and Crow beaks up and down, he just didn't know what to do. In that moment, the fight drained right out of him. He released an exasperated hoot, withdrew his talons and with a sweep of his wings shook Kuper off. He swooped low and to his right through the branches of a big pine to discourage followers and disappeared into the woods, probably returning to his roost in the cottonwoods, where he could rest and recuperate and think twice about ever hunting Crow again.

Exhausted and hurt, Kyp and Kuper dropped to the branches of a fir and settled, panting. For a long moment they allowed their wings to droop by their sides and simply gulped in lungfuls of air. Suddenly, Kuper, bleeding from the leg and the neck, bruised on the wing and shoulder, threw his head back and laughed.

"*That,*" Kuper chuckled, "was some pretty, *pretty* flying."

"Why, for the *love* of the Maker," Kyp exploded, "didn't

must be performed. Newlings are summoned and given Clan names. The Offering is presented. If there are judgments to be argued, the Family is convened. The fourth day is set aside for those games and sports particular to the Gathering: the relays and long flights. Fifth and sixth days are devoted to matters between Clans. Seventh day is spent in prayer and remembrance of those who have passed during the year. The eighth day marks the Long Story, followed by the invocation of the Maker's blessing. That done, families and bachelor units separate and make their way to the nesting grounds till fall.

Following the judgment on Kyp, a dark cloud had hung over the Gathering. There was less laughter than usual, fewer late-night conversations. Instead, small groups retreated to out-of-the-way perches to review things privately. It was more than just Kyp's departure, although with his departure, the interest in the games was considerably diminished — he was simply the best the Kinaar had to offer. Everyone had to face how close the Family had come to Splitting, and Splitting is a serious matter. It divides brother from sister, mother from son, cousins and nieces. Often, once a Family has split, generations can pass before the two groups speak again. The most famous example of this is when the Ketaka Family split. The Kutu Clan withdrew following charges and counter charges of cowardice regarding the driving off of an eagle, and no member of that group spoke to the rest of their Family for more than ten generations.

And while the Gathering continued, what of Kyp? How was he faring? Kyp spent most of his exile among the ravines and coulees that fed into the valley of the beaver dam. Kuper visited when he could, and in the meantime Kyp thought his solitary thoughts. He explored. There were discoveries to be made daily, even in as small a space as he confined himself to: Where could the best and safest bath be had? What trees offered the best cover? Which the best view? Time dragged for Kyp, and he spent it becoming expert in the ways of that valley.

His second day away, he circled a bushy jack pine, then dropped and perched on a branch a third of the way up. He pushed past the thick prickly outer mantle and moved in along a branch to the quiet, cooler hidden recesses nearer the trunk. High up on the protected east side of the tree, he'd stored a cache, the remains of a long-tailed weasel. Just as he had begun to feed, he heard something.

The bruises and scratches from his encounter with the horned owl were still fresh, so Kyp was especially cautious. Quiet as a spider spins, he set his salvage down on the branch and crept as close as he could to the tree trunk. He scanned the surroundings beyond the green-brown canopy of needles and twigs. Nothing moved in the air or stirred in the neighboring trees.

Then Kyp heard the sound once more. A slight scratching. Or a shifting. It was barely audible — but it was close. As he tried to determine the sound's origin, the weasel carcass slithered off the perch and tumbled down, head over tail, branch by branch, through the tree until it snagged on a broken twig and quietly swung there.

Kyp held his breath and waited. Still nothing moved. He dropped cautiously from one branch to the next. Near the bottom of the tree, only two or three branches from ground level, he heard the sound again. It was coming from a spot beneath him and to the right. He couldn't conceive of anything coming *up* a tree that he would be happy to greet, so he prepared to take the weasel carcass and fly — but his curiosity caught him and prodded him forward along the sloping lower branch.

Nothing. Nothing but shadows amid clumps of pine needles and cones and swaying grasses. Then, as his eyes adjusted to the gloom, something popped into focus. Hidden among the dried needles and scrub grasses, in the shadows of the tree's very lowest and largest branch, something crouched. Every instinct urged Kyp to flee.

He dropped down another branch, crept closer, pushed a twig aside.

There, in the dim shadows, squatted Kym, peering off in

the opposite direction, looking as if *she* too was hiding.

"What," Kyp asked, scanning the distance for whatever *she* might be hiding from, "are *you* doing here?"

Kym snapped her head about. "*Shh.* Go away."

Kyp stepped forward, careless of the branch that sprang back as he passed. "What do you mean?"

Kym snorted impatiently. "How much explaining is needed to understand 'Go Away'? It means Go. Away."

"I cached food here," he said, and held up the carcass he had recovered.

"Yes," Kym replied, her eyes still on something beyond the tree. "I see that."

"So, I was here first. *You* go away."

Kym clicked her beak in frustration and bobbed her head. "I'm not interested in your *food* —"

"You're not even supposed to have any contact with me."

"I'm not, you chucklehead," she snapped. "*You're* having contact with *me.*"

"How can *I* have contact with *you*," Kyp said, and took a step forward, "without *you* having contact with *me*?"

Exasperated, Kym turned on him. "*First!* I'm saying *first.* You had contact with me first. *You* spoke. *You* flopped down here."

"*I* came to check my cache." He shook the dangling carcass by its tail as proof.

"Fine! Have it your way. Believe me, I'm not interested in

your stale old weasel carcass. I'm busy."

"Doing?"

"Nothing you'd be interested in — and you're interfering."

"I'm not interfering, I'm — why are you crouching?" Kyp took another step closer and tried to peek out from beneath the branches.

Kym blocked his way. "Could you make any *more* noise? Why not just fly to the top of the tree and *shout*? Please, lower your voice."

"Lower my voice?" He took a step to his right. "You're not even supposed to be talking to me."

"I'm not," she said, moving in front of Kyp again.

"Of course you are! How can you be talking to me without talking to me? What are you doing, if not talking to me?"

"*This is not a conversation*! I'm answering you! *You* landed beside me. *You* approached me. *I'm* sitting here minding my own business —"

"Which is?"

"Not yours! Now just go away. Shoo!"

"*Shoo*? Shoo!! I've got my cache here, and I'm going to eat it, so if anyone is going to 'shoo' it will have to be you."

But Kym showed no signs of shooing, so Kyp certainly wasn't going to, either. Instead, he plucked up his meal again. Kym turned her back, sat and continued gazing off in the direction of the beaver pond.

"Is there something out there?" Kyp asked between beakfuls. "A hawk? Owl?"

"No. No, there's not," she replied without a glance at him. "You're in absolutely no danger if you want to leave. Whenever you're ready, just ... *go.*"

"Not till you tell me what's going on. I don't want to take my food and just go flying out there, not knowing what's waiting for me."

"Why did you hide it here?" Kym snapped.

"Because no one comes here."

"*I do!* Obviously."

"I haven't seen you here before."

"Oh, please, eat, do whatever you want, just be quiet."

Kyp tore into his meal again. For a few moments, he nibbled in silence as Kym peered through the brush.

"Just tell me," he whispered, "why did you come here?"

Kym continued staring. At last she sighed heavily. "*If* I tell you, *then* will you leave me alone?"

"Yes."

She hesitated. "You promise?"

"Yes."

She hesitated another moment, then blurted, "To watch."

Kyp blinked. "Watch what?"

"Them." Kym nodded in the direction of the lake.

97

"Them? Who?"

"The humans. Over there."

"Humans? Here? Where?"

"Down *there*. In the bushes. Beside the beaver dam. Use your eyes. Two of them. A female and a male, mating partners, I think. Lying on their bellies, under the blue spruce."

Kyp edged nearer Kym and peered through the same opening. Halfway across the valley, two pairs of limbs were sticking out, sheathed in something gray green and blending almost perfectly with the surroundings.

"Ooooh. There they are," Kyp said, seeing them at last.

"*Now* you see them?" she asked slowly, as if questioning a newling.

"Yes." Kyp shook his head in wonder that he hadn't seen them earlier.

"Good."

"It's clever the way they've hidden themselves."

"Well, that's humans for you. They're inventive creatures."

Both stared at the humans, then Kyp spoke again. "Kuper says he's the only Crow who comes out here."

"Another Crow with weak powers of observation," Kym commented dryly. "And I see I'm not the only Crow you've spoken to."

"Ah, well, that is … See, *I* spoke to him. He never

approached me, it's completely my fault — and you're not going to tell anyone, are you?"

"Shh! No, it doesn't matter to me. I won't say anything." Kym glanced briefly at Kyp, then turned her attention back to the humans. "I didn't think it was right — the sentence you received — if that means anything to you. That little Klea wasn't your fault. I understand why Kalum pronounced judgment the way he did. He had to do something. There is too much bad blood between the Clans, but ... but that still doesn't make it right."

One of the humans slid forward and pushed itself up on its forelimbs.

"What are they doing?"

"That's the question, isn't it?" Kym murmured as much to herself as to Kyp.

"Well, let's fly down and find out."

"No, no, *no*. Shh. Stay put." She pushed Kyp back. "Watch. If you interfere, they'll stop doing whatever they're doing. If you look closely, you can see that the big one is pointing a black square thing with a long tube thing on the front of it."

Then Kyp saw that the human was holding something glossy and black. Immediately he raised his wings in alarm. "A stinging human!"

"No, no!" Kym hissed. "Just stay put and watch. It's not a stinger."

"How can you be certain?"

"I've seen them before. They point them." As if the human heard her, it raised the black object and pressed it closely to its face. "And then they wrap their paws around them. And, then, if you listen carefully …"

Through the still air, a slight, thin whirring sounded, like the thrumming of a partridge, followed by a pair of muffled clicks.

When Kym exhaled, Kyp realized that he had also been holding his breath.

"Did you hear it?" she asked.

"A noise like a cricket?"

"Yes!"

"What are they doing?"

"I don't know for sure. But they do it all the time. Pull that thing close to their face. Point. And then … *whirrrr, click, click.*"

"Is it harmful?"

"No, I don't think so," Kym answered with a quick shake of her head. "I've seen them do it to *themselves* too — even more than they do it to birds." She studied Kyp a moment, then made a quick decision. "I have a theory though."

"What?"

Kym lowered her voice, as though others might be listening. "I think it's courtship."

"What? That?"

"Yes, I think it's courting ritual."

"But you just said they do it to Crows — to us?"

"Well, after all, aren't humans jealous of Crows? Maybe they're jealous enough that they want a Crow mate —"

"A *Crow* mate??"

"It's just a theory."

"So … courtship?"

"Yes! I mean, don't *we* bring gifts of food when we court? Sometimes humans toss bits of food on the ground for us — I've seen it. And other animals have rituals of all sorts when they court, so why not humans?"

Kyp stared at the humans lying under the bush, their gangly limbs splayed out in the dirt. "That's a dumb idea," he snorted. "They're *huge*."

"How do you explain it then? Those black objects don't seem to *do* anything. Same with those black tubes humans press up against their faces, like two long eyes. See? Those two have a pair of *them*, too. The square black objects make a noise, the long eyes don't, but the humans put them on and take them off and point them at each other all the time. They don't seem afraid of them. So what else can it be?"

Kyp opened his beak to answer and then stopped to think. "Who knows?" he answered at last.

"*That's* just the problem. The frustrating, *agonizing* problem. I've been watching and watching and watching …

for so long. There's one mating couple that I've studied for years — and sometimes I think I haven't learned a thing." Kym sighed. "What do they do with those things? We may never know."

"We might," Kyp offered after a moment's thought.

"How?"

"Simple," he said, then leaped up and swung out into the air.

"No, no! Stop! Don't go any farther," Kym hissed, but Kyp was already beyond hearing. His outstretched wings took him to within a couple of wingspans of the human that had made the whirring noise. The human's face was still pressed firmly into the black square.

Kyp hovered and landed soft as an autumn leaf. He looked carefully at the first human. It was lying on its immense belly, its head sprouting a fringe of grayish fur. According to rumor, that made it the male of the species. Kyp hopped once, twice and was next to a black pouch. He grasped a flap in his beak and tugged. The flap emitted a soft ripping noise and a package slid out. The human stirred, disturbed by the sound. Kyp tensed and prepared to fly. Then the human drew the black box up and adjusted its face snugly into it. A whirring sound followed ... then two clicks.

Kyp lifted the heavy packet in his beak. It dangled and swung awkwardly, but he felt certain he would be able to fly with it. There was one other thing he had to know first, though.

He quietly set the packet down and hopped to the foot end of the male. Kyp was close enough to hear the soft gurglings and rumblings of the human's digestive system. Close enough to hear the quiet rush of each breath being drawn in and then exhaled. Kyp hopped closer. Now he was close enough to feel the warmth of the human's body radiate against his left wing, just a feather's breadth from the pair of long eyes that lay on the grass. Kyp craned forward, tipped his head down until he could look into the narrow end of the black glossy device. For a moment he saw nothing. Then ... in surprise he released a soft croak. The human shifted.

Kyp glanced over just as the human removed the black box from its face. He skipped back to the bag and plucked up the soft package that had fallen out. The human was rising now and making throaty noises of surprise and alarm. This must have relayed some message because the second human lunged. Kyp grasped the corner of the packet and flung himself into the air. The packet was awkward and threw him off balance, and both humans were advancing, making angry growling sounds. A quick beat of his wings carried him up and out of reach. Fearing the loud boom of a human stinger, he flew without glancing back.

Now Kym sprang into the air, diving low over the

humans' heads to divert their attention. The humans ducked and threw up their arms. Kyp flew past the fir tree, across the water to a distant spruce that would offer a view if the humans chose to follow. He laid the package out on a thick branch nearest the trunk and drew a welcome lungful of air. It was only then he realized how hard he had exerted himself. Across the water, the humans were still shouting and gesturing. Kyp laughed — and was still laughing when Kym landed beside him.

"That was *so* stupid," Kym scolded. "Do you *know* how stupid that was? It goes beyond stupid. You make a *sparrow* look smart. A Crow that was just stupid would be a genius beside you."

"You know what my father used to say?" Kyp said between laughs. "Something is stupid only when it doesn't work. *That* worked."

"So, what did you think you were doing?"

"Exploring. And hunting. I've captured scavenge from the humans. Do you want some?"

Kym dipped her head over the loot. "I could eat," she allowed.

"Well then. Good eating," Kyp said and set to.

"Of course," Kym said between beakfuls, "you'll have to perform prayer and purification."

"Of course."

"Can I ask what you were looking at beside the human?"

Kyp glanced up from his meal. "Do you want to know?"

"Agh! Of course, I want to … *yes*, I want to know! Why would I ask if I didn't want to know?" She took a deep breath and tried to calm herself. "You are so frustrating. Are you always like this?"

Kyp swallowed his food and cocked his head. "I looked into the long eyes."

Kym hopped forward. "No!"

"Yes."

"*Really*? What did you see?"

"You won't believe me."

"I might." She paused. "So? What?"

"No. You'll think I'm lying."

"Did they …" Kym lowered her voice and leaned forward. "… make things seem closer?"

Kyp's eyes widened. "*Yes!* Everything looked bigger! How did you know?"

"I had a theory. I mean, why would they look through them unless they changed the way they saw? What did you see?"

"I peeked through the opening on the smaller end —"

"And?"

"And the *entire* other side of the valley — everything — the trees, the grass, the bushes, even the bugs seemed ten times bigger."

"That must have been incredible."

"It was *amazing*! And a little scary."

"I can understand that."

They ripped into the package of human salvage as they chattered — tomatoes, some of that pale, spongy substance that humans squish things between, thin strips of meat — but they paid little attention to the food, so intent were they on their conversation.

"They look at us all the time, you know," Kym continued, her beak still half full.

"What do you mean?" Kyp pulled a piece of meat out of the bag.

"I've seen them putting on the long eyes. They'll do it to look at us. But *only* when we're at a distance."

"And that would make us seem —"

"Closer. Yes."

Kyp cocked his head and tried to imagine a human placing the long eyes on and then pointing them at him. "Why would they do that?"

"What do you mean?"

"Why would they want to see us up close?"

"Well. It *must* mean they're interested in us. I know you think the courtship idea isn't likely, but that's how I first started thinking that the long eyes must make things bigger. I reasoned that if they use the long eyes when we're at a distance, it must mean they do something over a distance. If courtship was involved, it would all make sense. *Wanting* to see someone. *Wanting* to see them up close." Kym abruptly stopped eating and began a quick self-grooming. "Anyway. I should go. I'll have purification to do, too, after eating the human salvage."

Crumbs of the human food were scattered about the branch, and ants had swarmed around them, performing cleanup. Kyp eyed the scurrying insects and plucked one up. "You know," he said as he swallowed the ant, "you really shouldn't come back here anymore."

Kym stopped in the middle of grooming. "Pardon me?"

"If someone was to find out that you'd been here, at the same time as I was, you could risk —"

"Excuse me? Have you heard a word I've said to you? I *am* coming back — have no doubt about that — and if other Crows can't understand why, that's their problem. I know why I come here, and believe me, it's not for *you*."

"I know that. I never said that."

"And if someone was to ask me — and they won't, why would they? No one ever comes out this way — I would tell them why. And if they couldn't understand, *that* would be their problem."

Suddenly the branch bent. They turned their heads and saw Kuper folding his wings.

Clutched in his talons was an enormous slab of what appeared to be a fresh kill. "Hi," he said, looking from Kyp to Kym.

"Hi," replied Kyp as he tried to figure out what to do next. "Kuper, you know Kym, right?"

The big Crow stayed at the end of the branch, dropped his piece of meat and looked at Kym. "Good eating," he said, rather formally.

"Good eating," she replied.

The two continued to look one at the other. "I met Kym when I went looking for a cache of mine," Kyp explained. "She didn't know I was here."

Neither Kym nor Kuper seemed ready to say anything, so Kyp turned to Kym. "Kuper helped me find this place. He's not going to tell anyone about … about any of this. Right?"

"No more than she would," Kuper allowed.

"There you go then."

An uncomfortable silence hovered as each considered the other two. Then Kym skipped to the end of a branch. "I have to go. There's a Naming at the Gathering that I should attend. I'll see you both later." As she leaped from the branch and swooped over the water, Kyp and Kuper stared after her. Her reflection sped across the shimmering surface below her as if there were two identical bodies, perfectly synchronized.

So there you have three young, headstrong Crows — all in direct contravention of judgment: Kym and Kuper, for speaking to someone under Eviction. Kyp for breaking

Eviction, and for talking with others while under judgment. Hardly good role models, any of them. And yet, I tell you now, without these three, it's not certain that any of us would have survived this Gathering.

CHAPTER 14

Now I must take you on a short detour, and I don't wish to lose any of you in an updraft. Perch close and listen patiently. Among us are those who envy the human. Know this, Cousins, it is the *human* who envies *us*.

Back in First Times, humans and Crows were the same size, and humans, like Crows, had fine long wings that sprang where their scrawny limbs do today. Built for fast flight, humans were like your peregrines, and they were always busy.

Even back then, however, nothing could fly as pretty as a Crow, and though humans were fast, it was Great Crow who was most beloved among all animals. Great Crow loved to entertain with stories and jokes. At night, when creatures slept, it was near the roost of Great Crow. First Human blew back and forth, always busy, but inside, First Human was empty. No matter how busy he got, no matter how quickly he flew, nothing filled that emptiness. One day he made a plan. I will challenge Great Crow, he thought, to a competition of flight. Then I will become something important.

The Maker, though, knows our thoughts before they form in our heads. She flew to Great Crow's perch and sat with him.

"My friend," she said, "listen. The Human has been fretting and will soon ask all creation to judge who is the master of the air."

Great Crow chuckled to himself when he heard this, but felt his feathers rise. He bobbed his head and honed his beak against a branch. "How dare he?" he asked the Maker. "The outcome is certain. Tell me — who curls through the air and performs loops and somersaults?"

"You do," the Maker replied.

"Who drops from the heavens straight as hail, then draws up at the last moment?"

"You do," the Maker answered patiently. "But mind me, Great Crow," she said and frowned, "I want no trouble. You and all creatures are my family and are precious to me. I advise you to avoid this quarrel. Go away to the north country. Stay there for a time. Eat fish and caribou until this notion of First Human's has passed."

Reluctantly, Great Crow nodded his agreement, but inside he fumed. When the Maker left, he hopped up and down on the branch and thought, Of all the insolence! Why should *I* be forced to move because of First Human's folly? Why should *I* fly to the cold, barren north country? Why should *I* disappear, with no explanation, as though I am a coward?

Ignoring the Maker's wishes was impossible, unthinkable. But the shame and frustration Great Crow felt as he considered what the other creatures would whisper put him in such a state that the only sensible option seemed to first take a nap.

While Great Crow slept away his irritation, First Human arrived. He flew three circuits around the sleeping Crow, then called down his challenge. Startled, Great Crow awoke but didn't reply — just stuck his head farther under his wing, trying to think what he should do. First Human repeated his challenge louder. If Great Crow wouldn't accept the contest, he announced, everyone would know he was afraid. Great Crow felt his feathers rising, but — remembering the Maker's advice — didn't answer.

Then First Human made his terrible wager. "Whoever loses," he called, "will be known forever as a coward, too weak to support the weighty privilege of flight.

Whoever loses," he continued, "must give up their wings forever."

Great Crow opened one eye. Everyone knows that nothing can fly like a Crow. He accepted.

Every creature large and small was invited to watch. First Human began. He flew so quickly, he arrived back at the perch before his own shadow. He flew so quickly, he was returning to the branch before he'd even left. Shouts and howls of praise erupted! All creatures admired the speed that First Human demonstrated in this, his fastest flight.

Then it was Great Crow's turn. He dropped from the branch and unfurled his wings — and it was as though flight had been invented for the first time. Was ever there anything so graceful? The delicate foam edging the crest of an incoming wave looked coarse in comparison. The dew gracing the leaf at dawn looked drab. Great Crow flew so sweetly that every other flight was instantly forgotten. There could be no question. The competition was unanimously decided in favor of Great Crow, and First Human, true to his word, relinquished his wings.

So First Human was defeated in a competition that should never have happened, but try as he might, Great Crow couldn't contain his scorn or be a gracious winner. He circled above First Human, laughing and whooping. He swooped, taunted and sang rude songs.

That's when the Maker appeared. And, oh, she was angry.

"Great Crow," she called as the skies grew darker. "Great fool! Become smaller." And in that moment, Great Crow shrunk and shrunk until he became the size we are today. Frightened and shamed in front of everyone, Great Crow flew away as the Maker pronounced the remaining judgment.

"Human, since you insisted on this wager, stay earthbound and busy. Make things, shape things, plant things and grow gardens. Great Crow," she called, turning her attention to the retreating figure, "stay small and let size temper your pride. Let Humans chase you from their gardens, but let wings, the source of your pride and error, keep you safe to the end of time. Use flight to save your life and your wits to protect your family."

Because Great Crow remained close to the Maker's heart, however, she also called a final blessing after him. "Small you will remain, but move as a group and find strength in that group. Let your numbers be your security and comfort, and use your voice to call warning so none can ever take you by surprise."

And since First Times, that is the way things have been.

Humans alone are creatures fallen from flight. Since those long-ago First Times, the human has truly become a creature of the earth, with a soul and heart rooted in the earth. Everything about humans now is earthlike, heavy and stone hard. They resent us for the loss they suffered and hate all animals because they were witnesses to their shame. And they are busy every moment of every day trying to find some way to avenge themselves.

This is how things have been since First Times, conflict between humans and Crows. With each gain made, there is always a loss. We steal from the humans, and when they can, they kill us.

I remind you of this now because humans play an important role in this Telling, and we must remember how we came to our relationship with them.

And as we speak of the human, know this too. Though the Maker took away their power of flight, humans have grown powerful in a manner that is hard for us to comprehend. Once there were no more humans on Earth than there are foxes or weasels. Once you could fly the entire six of the day from dawn to sunset and never see a human or a human's roost. "Back before eggs," as my mother used to say, back before humans built roosts on every hill and paths through every valley, the most abundant creature was the buffalo. Their herds were so immense that dust rose in clouds as they moved. It was as though an ocean of hair and hoof and horn swept over the hills and filled the plains.

This is truth, recollected by my elders who heard it from theirs, and I have seen with my own eyes the last remnants of those great herds. In times past, we followed buffalo, for insects fed upon them, and birds fed upon the insects, and wolves and coyotes and bears hunted both the buffalo and the creatures that followed the buffalo — so wherever the buffalo passed, there was good eating.

It is said that we Crows first began the northerly migrations to follow the buffalo to their fresh meadows. Those times are gone. The buffalo have disappeared, killed by humans, whose roosts crowd the plains as the buffalo once did. Now it is the humans and their great caches of food and their animal servants and their fields of grain and fruit that provide for us.

There is this difference though. The buffalo allowed others to follow and flourish: the black fly and prairie dog, the coyote and rabbit. But where *humans* gather, all other creatures diminish. Only those things thrive that eat what the human eats — have the speed to steal it and the craft to escape. So, while we often rely on humans, we view them with a mixed heart.

It's said that back in First Times, all creatures could speak to one another. I believe one day it will be like that again. Then the divisions between us will melt and human and Crow will perch together.

In the meantime, we live in the world as it is. Because the human is deadly, we limit our contact and purify and pray after each encounter. Because the human can extinguish something as abundant as the buffalo, we must always be watchful. These laws made regarding the human are made for a reason.

Hold these thoughts in one empty talon for later, and grasp our previous story with the other.

Where was Kyp on the third day of his Eviction? Hidden like a sandpiper in the reeds and rushes near the river. *What* was he doing there? Watching cautiously, making certain that he couldn't be seen. What was he watching? His Family. Us.

Nothing is missed so much as when it is forbidden. Nothing seems so precious as those things you cannot have. Never mind that there were only a few days left of Kyp's Eviction. Never mind that he had spent time with both Kym and Kuper. When the sun dropped and night fell, he felt as lost as the last mosquito of autumn. Each moment away from the Family seemed like a thousand moments. Finally, when his every waking moment became consumed with thoughts of the Gathering and his comrades, Kyp decided to take things in talon. Cautiously, he flew to the base of the cliffs upon which the Gathering Tree grew. There, amid the bulrushes and mud and small biting flies, he watched his brother and sister Crows soar in and out. Did this make things better?

No, of course not! It made them a hundred times worse. It made him miss his friends. It made him miss the ceremonies and games. It made him miss grooming and preening. He recalled the casual conversation that springs up between Crows as they rest together on a common perch or hunt for bugs in the grass and felt its loss.

As Kyp crouched in those rushes and scrub, feeling sorry for himself, a group of six young Crows flew close overhead. To avoid being seen, Kyp dropped to nearly ground level. He watched the youngsters fly overhead and felt a fierce spasm of envy and sadness.

At that precise moment, a gust of warm air struck him. This was peculiar. There, under the cover of brush, and at the base of a hill, if anything, he should have felt cool, damp air. The warm air swept past again, and he captured the scent of … he couldn't bring to mind what, but something familiar. He glanced down. There, almost hidden by bushes, was the opening to a human-made tunnel.

Kyp had seen things of this sort in the past. Great stone tubes that snaked underground beneath the human nesting grounds and emptied into the river. Of course, he saw objects made by humans every day — how could he not? — and never thought much about them, but after his last conversation with Kym, he was inclined to view things differently. He stepped closer. He listened and hopped up on a branch to inspect the tunnel. Its mouth was half covered by the tough, thorny branches of a sprawling rosebush. He ducked beneath the bush and peered straight down the dank mouth. He called once, softly, jumped to another branch and waited. Nothing.

He lingered another moment, the branch still bobbing beneath his talons, then spread his wings and dropped a short distance into the tunnel's mouth. Gravel crunched as he landed. Again, that smell teased him. He peered as far as he could up the shaft. It opened around him like an immense cavernous mouth. One could see some by the dim reflected light, but not much and not far. Kyp hesitated a moment — then hopped into the dark.

The eerie feelings that the underground conjures up have ancient origins, and Kyp knew that to proceed was forbidden. He knew that snakes lived underground, and weasels. He knew coyotes and foxes dug their dens into hillsides. Still, he felt an urge to continue.

The tunnel floor was smooth and dry, except for the thinnest trickle of water that meandered in tiny loops through clumps of dust and debris.

Kyp moved hesitantly, hopping with his curious hitch-legged gait, skipping forward three or four steps, then stopping to listen and stare. Every tap, every rustle echoed. He raised his beak and sniffed the air. Again, just beyond recognition, was something.

There was a curious thing about the tunnel. Every one or two hundred hops, a small upward-slanting shaft pierced the ceiling, connecting the tunnel to the surface and open air.

Some light and the odd sound entered through these holes. Taking some comfort from this connection to the surface, Kyp moved forward faster.

Side tunnels branched off in different directions, but the stream trickled from the passage that sloped up and to his left. He followed it, hopping through one patch of light into darkness, and then approaching the next patch of light. As Kyp came around a bend, he noticed a fresh pile of loose gravel. Directly above the pile a jagged crack fractured the roof like a dark scar splitting the rock. Through the fissure, a stream of sharp-smelling water trickled. Kyp recognized the smell at last — sulfur! He dipped his talons in the stream and felt the water run hot. The gap widened near the roof of the tunnel, with just enough space for a Crow to slip through if he wasn't too plump. Up Kyp leaped and cautiously squeezed within.

There are times when everything you have imagined in all your imaginings falls short of what you encounter. Kyp had prepared himself for impenetrable darkness, for the sense of panic that comes with close confinement. Instead, on the other side of the tunnel, by the faint half-light that filtered through the crack, he could make out the dim outline of an immense cavern that dropped away and stretched on for what seemed like forever. Great spiraling columns of stone surged out of the gloom. Glossy beaks of rock stabbed down. Crystals shimmered and flickered in the walls and from the roof, and everywhere steam and shadow rose and swirled. It was the most terrifying, soul-inspiring, wonderful thing Kyp had ever encountered. He struggled between wanting to escape as quickly as possible and needing to explore farther.

Who made this cavern? Not humans, that much was certain. The things humans craft are regularly shaped and run directly from point to point to point. There was nothing *direct* about any of this. The cavern sloped and twisted and gyrated. It billowed from narrow confines into expansive chambers and then slithered back into tiny perfect wedges. At one time, there must have been a true river running underground — the cavern's enormous size attested to it. Long years of wear had formed the cave and polished its glistening walls. At some point, things had changed, however. Now, what little water there was gathered in pools and emerged as a tiny stream that approached and then spilled over the lip of the crack in the tunnel.

Kyp crouched, open-beaked with wonder, turning and then turning again, gazing at this strange new world of stone, water and vapor. But, as the saying goes, "Every hole has its badger." And this was no exception.

Now, your chickadees and meadowlarks and other such creatures can live on talk alone, but we've perched long enough. It's late, and the darkness is pressing close. I'm

PART TWO

CHAPTER 15

Move in.

Now that you've returned, move in. There is room on these branches, and it's best at this time of deep night if we stay close to one another.

Everyone move in and, for a moment, open your eyes. Use the moonlight provided by the Maker, and look about you. Consider the cousin next to you and realize this. Each relationship you share, even if just for this brief time spent listening on a common perch in the middle of the night, is precious. Nothing proves this more than the devastating happenings of these past few days.

Cousins, it is said that the Maker sang creation into being. She sang sacred words and Great Crow appeared. She continued her song and the dusky night sky, the flickering stars and the first feathery clouds emerged. When finally she rested her voice, the great world nest was formed. The Telling is a kind of creation as well. It is the way we Crows shape who we are. It is our history, our guide, our conscience, a reflection of ourselves in the pool of eternity as we glide past. It is the towering trunk that rises through the length of our Family Tree, up to the end of all things and back through the canopy of time, down to the very roots of all things, where Great Crow and the Maker abide. Each story we tell or hear nourishes another branch on this immense, aged and many-limbed testament to our Family. So, now, let me continue this Telling — from our migration along the coast, through to the trial, the Eviction, to this precise moment when we find ourselves listening. Listening to a voice, a single voice, shouting:

"What are you *doing* hanging around here?"

The voice was Kym's, and there was no mistaking the annoyance in it. As she fluttered down beside a surprised Kyp, her throat feathers bristled.

Kyp tried — unsuccessfully — to appear unconcerned. "I just wanted to see what was going on."

"Do you even *understand* what Eviction means?" Kym hissed, trying to keep her voice low. "Do you understand what the punishment is if you are seen by a member of the Family?"

"I just thought —"

"Banishment. *Permanent* exile. Not just a few days' eviction. Forever. And then you're just another ragged Outcast. Is that what you want?"

"I won't get caught." Kyp moved farther into the scrub.

"*I* saw you."

"That's different."

"*How* is that different?" Kym snapped her beak in frustration. "I don't have any better eyes than the others."

"I meant for you to see me."

Caught unawares, Kym stopped, her beak open. "*Why*, for the love of the Maker?" she sputtered.

Kyp remained silent a moment and then muttered, "I wanted to know what's going on up there."

Kym rolled her eyes and sighed. When at last she spoke, it was in the slow, exaggerated way one might use with a particularly dim newling. "It doesn't matter what's going on, Kyp. You. Can't. Be seen. Here."

"I can't stand it anymore. I mean, you and Kuper are good about visiting. But I should be up *there*, at the Gathering —"

Kym cut him off. "That's not possible. You have only a couple more days left in your Eviction. Now, go. Please."

Kyp glanced up the hill once more as though he might catch a glimpse of the Gathering Tree and the flight contests. At last he shrugged. "All right. But I want to show you something first."

"Are you joking? I can't be seen with you."

"No, it's — It won't take long. I've found a place I think you should see."

"A place? Where?"

"Follow me."

"Can you tell me a little more —"

Now it was Kyp who cut Kym off. "It'd take longer to tell than to look. It's not far. Come on."

They skimmed low, skirting the grasses and scrub, and came upon a little ravine, felt the cool air blow up off it. Kyp continued to drop.

Near the bottom of the ravine, on the south-facing wall, were some bushes. Behind the bushes was a shadow.

Kym stopped well short of the tunnel and leaped up several times before finally settling. She glanced at the cave and then at Kyp. "Yes?"

"It's a cave. Humans made it."

"Yes. They make a number of these. Although …" The two advanced on the entrance. The smooth gray rock was cold to the touch. Kym eyed the tunnel's entrance. The dusky shadows extended far back. "… this one seems to have been abandoned. Or maybe it's unused. There's something funny about it."

"Why dig into the earth and then just … leave it? Do you think someone lived here?"

"I don't think so. It's old. There's no smell of human that I can detect. Can you?"

"No. Maybe it's an abandoned roost."

Kym shook her head. "No, humans don't live in this sort of thing."

"*Sometimes* they live underground."

"I know, but they make cubes to roost in, above ground or below. This is like a long tube."

"Then what is it for?"

"I don't know, for certain."

The two sat a moment, just peering at the brooding, incomprehensible tunnel. "You know what?" Kyp blurted at last.

"What?"

"I've been in there."

"Right." Kym glanced at him to see if this was a joke. "Really?"

"Quite a ways."

Kym shook her head. "Underground?"

"Well, yes."

Her eyes widened. "What were you thinking? That's not allowed —"

"I know, but —"

"— *and* it's dangerous," she continued. "Which is why it's

forbidden. There could be any kind of groundling. Snakes. Rats. Racoons."

"I was listening as I went. It's quiet."

"It doesn't matter how quiet it is. It's forbidden. You know that. If Uncle Kork or Kyrk heard … You're either very brave or very stupid. Or both."

Kyp took a few short hops closer to the entrance. "Do you want to go in?"

Kym snorted with exasperation. "Did you just hear me? It's forbidden, so, no, I don't want to go in. I most definitely do not. Is there anything you do that's *not* forbidden? Do you even understand what the word means? I hope you performed purification —"

"Of course I did."

"Now, look, we've got to leave. If someone sees you, there'll be trouble. It's probably better if I fly with you, so if anyone looks, they'll see two Crows."

"You shouldn't risk it," Kyp objected.

"I'll go with you as far as the beaver dam."

"All right." Kyp turned away from the tunnel. "I just thought you were interested in human things."

"I am. And thanks. But we should go. We'll keep to the bushes. If we fly above the river, someone will spot us."

They skimmed along the ground until they had slipped around the bend in the river. Then, when they were sure no one was watching, they quickly cut across the water.

Kyp landed heavily in the big willow that dominated the valley. Kym came to rest close beside him.

"I'm sorry I wasted your time," Kyp said. "I thought you'd like seeing it."

"I'm interested in humans but — go *underground*? I don't think so." Kym dipped her head to adjust her wing feathers. "How was it? Was it scary?"

"A little," Kyp allowed, "but you know what? Every hundred or so hops, humans have sunk holes into the top of the tunnel and capped them with a crisscross of flat stone. I don't know what they put the holes in for — you can't get through them because of the crisscrossing stones — but they let in some light. And the most amazing thing I saw? I don't think it was built by the humans at all."

"What?"

"You turn one corner and high up near the top of one tunnel there's a crack about two Crows wide. If you go in there —"

"You went in *there*?"

"Yes. Sure."

Kym stared at him a moment, then shook her head. "I don't get you. So, is there any light when you go through this crack?"

"Some. A little. I mean, *very* little, but the thing is, it's … If only you could go in and see it. The walls *glitter*. Branches of twisted stone hang down and spikes poke up. There's

131

rock that's polished smooth as the surface of water, and it seems to flow like water, too, and the cave itself, well, it stretches out for, for ... I don't know how far. You can't imagine the end of it, that's how far."

Kym listened carefully. "That does sound ... remarkable. But if I can give you a word of advice, don't mention it for some time after you return. I don't think anyone will be impressed to know that during your Eviction for breaking the rules, you spent your time breaking other rules."

Kyp was silent a moment as he considered this, then he spoke again. "But?"

"But?"

"Why? That's the thing that bothers me."

"Why what?"

"Why do humans do it? Is the cavern part of the tunnel? Why build the tunnel at all? And why build it from up in the hillside to down by the river? There aren't any humans living here."

Kym squeezed a piece of bark absently between her talons. "I would say the only reason for having a ... thing ... like that would be to carry rainwater from one place to another."

Kyp thought about it. "Why would you want to do that? If it's raining in one place, wouldn't it be raining in the other place too?"

"It might not. It could be a very small shower. Or what

if you were thirsty and you didn't have water where you were?"

"Then you would just go somewhere else."

"Yes — if you can fly. Humans can't. It takes them forever to waddle anywhere on their hind legs, so it might make sense to have a tunnel thing to carry water."

"But there's a river down here if they want to drink. And, anyway, humans don't drink from the tunnel when it rains."

"True. And they don't come to wash, either. So maybe there's too much water in one place, and they have to move it. Or maybe there's water that they don't want, a different kind of water. Or maybe they do something with the water, and then they don't want it anymore, so they take the water from up there and send it down. That might be —" She gave a short shake of her wings. "*See?*"

"See what?"

"*That's* the thing about humans! You *think* you've got them figured out, you *think* you know them, and then they do something like this, and — bang! — you have to begin all over again."

The sound of a twig snapping broke the silence. Two humans slipped under a branch and walked along the lakeshore. Kym fixed her eyes intently upon them.

"Look at them," she said. The humans were ordinary enough, as far as humans went. One taller and thinner, one shorter and stockier. Both encased in the skins that humans drape on their bodies. "They're like a puzzle or a riddle, and every time you return to it, there's more to discover. I could watch them and watch them and never get enough."

The humans approached more closely, ambling aimlessly and grunting as they often seemed to.

"Watch this," Kym said and repeated the sounds they were making. The humans stopped and looked about, craning their heads, looking high and low, then walked on again. Again, Kym mimicked their sounds. This time they stared — directly at Kym.

Kym repeated the sound. The humans stood stock-still. It was clear the noise — whatever it meant — was having a profound effect on them.

Kyp looked at her. "I'm not sure this is a good idea." But Kym ignored him, repeating the sound.

The humans drew nearer, cocking their heads and squinting at Kym. One of them released a complicated series of clicks and grunts. Kym repeated it grunt for grunt, the feathers around her neck and up and down her back rising.

"Kym," Kyp hissed, "what if —"

Then Kym did an extraordinary thing. She swooped to the ground, landed on the grass in front of the humans, no more than twenty Crows from them, and repeated the sounds. The humans made the sounds again. So did Kym.

By now, the feathers on Kyp's back and shoulders were

rising. The humans crouched. One of them made a new sound, and Kym repeated it, then turned and looked up at Kyp.

"Now watch this," she called, and said, "Hello." The humans stared intently. "Hello," Kym repeated. This time, one of the humans, the smaller one, opened its lips and a sound emerged that could have been, if you were generous, "Hello" in Crow.

The sound struck Kyp like thunder. He peered down at the humans and then at Kym. "Did it just do what I thought it did?"

Kym turned to Kyp. "Yes! They can be taught to repeat certain words. I've done this before. Humans can learn three or four simple phrases if I —"

"Look out!" Kyp shouted and launched himself from his perch. One of the humans had quietly removed one of the soft floppy skins it had draped over its body and, while Kym's attention was on Kyp, had suddenly thrown the skin in Kym's direction. It had intended to cover and then capture Kym, but at Kyp's warning, Kym jumped up and flew clear.

As the one threw the skin, both humans leaped forward, stretching their long upper limbs to seize Kym. Kyp streaked in low over their heads, and the humans flung their talons up at him. He darted in and around the flailing limbs and plucked a hair from the top of the larger one's head. A

135

howl emerged from its gaping mouth as Kyp and Kym sped to the safety of a nearby pine. As Kym flew, she tossed another human word behind her that apparently held some power. The humans stopped chasing and speaking and were seemingly struck dumb.

"Well," Kyp said as he settled on the long, wide lower limb of the pine. "How smart was that?"

"That's the thing," Kym said between gasps, "about humans. You never know. What they will do. Until they do it. Sometimes they throw food to you. Sometimes they try to grab you. They're completely. Completely. Unpredictable." The way she said it almost made it sound like a good thing.

"So, you've done that a number of times?"

Kym simply nodded, still trying to catch her breath. "Many."

"One of these times they'll catch you."

"No, they're too slow," she argued half-heartedly before returning to something more interesting. "But you know what? Sometimes I can get humans to repeat fifteen, even sixteen words."

Kyp eyed Kym. She didn't appear to be boasting, but the idea of humans mastering even one beakful of words seemed out of the question. "Really?"

"Really."

Kyp looked at the humans as they gathered their things

and lumbered off. How dim they seemed as they loped about.

"But do you think they *understand* any of it?"

Kym remained silent a moment, as though considering something, and then said, "I don't know. I almost believe they can."

"Can I ask you something?"

"Yes."

"It's kind of private."

"I'm here, aren't I? I'm talking to you when I'm not supposed to be — I think that makes everything we say private."

Kyp looked directly at Kym. "What do you think of Kuper?"

The expression she returned was impenetrable. "Why are you asking?"

"Because he asked me to," Kyp replied. "Just after you left the other day."

"Kuper? He's nice," she offered quietly. "Seems kind of a loner. Why?"

"He likes you."

Kym snorted. "I don't think so."

"He does."

"Why doesn't he say anything to me then?"

"He thinks …" Kyp turned his attention to the branch. "He thinks I can say something he can't. I don't know."

"Well," she said after a moment, "maybe you can."

Kyp stared at Kym. "What's that supposed to mean?"

"It means I've got to go," she said abruptly and leaped from the branch. "I'm supposed to babysit my Aunty's yearling."

"But what did that mean?" Kyp called after Kym again, but she was already winging over the river.

As Kym disappeared into the distance, Kyp grew aware of another presence. From a tree farther up the valley, a solitary figure lifted, glided to the pine and alighted.

"Kuper?" Kyp looked at the big bird with surprise. "Why didn't you join us?"

"I just caught dinner. Some?" he inquired and draped a squirrel carcass over the branch. "So? Did you get to talk to Kym about me?" he asked as he plucked up a beakful of meat.

"Yes."

"What did she say?"

"She said she likes you."

Kuper appeared to study two ducks as they swooped down and landed with a splash in the beaver pond. "Was that all?" he asked. "Did she say anything else?"

"Nothing much. We didn't talk that long."

Kuper returned his attention to Kyp. "Can you take something to her the next time you see her?"

"Like what?"

"I've a gift I want —"

"Take it to her yourself."

"Couldn't you just ... present it to her?"

"I don't —"

"*You* talk to her. Tell her I'm thinking of her. Give her the gift. Can you do that?" The big Crow stared earnestly at Kyp.

"If you can't *talk* to her —" Kyp shook his head. "If you can't even take the gift, what's the point?"

"I just ... I'm not good at that sort of thing."

"What makes you think I am?"

"I've watched you. You know your way around the Flock. You know how to talk to them. I've spent too long on my own."

"Excuse me? Have you noticed that *I'm* evicted?"

"Oh, that." Kuper shrugged dismissively. "That's simply the older ones using you as an example for the youngsters. You'll recover from this in no time — and be even more popular. I feel that if you can get her to ... to see me in a different way. If you can just get things going between us, then it'll be okay. I'll be able to talk to her if I know that ... she wants to ... talk with me. You know?"

"Well," Kyp replied doubtfully, "not really. You want to court her, right?"

"No," Kuper said matter-of-factly and tore off another strip of meat. "I want *you* to court her. For me."

"But, but that doesn't make sense. It should be coming from you."

"Take it from me," the big bird said dryly. "It would be *much* better coming from you. Look at me."

Kuper threw his wings open. Kyp cocked his head and surveyed him.

"You look —"

"I'm a galoot. I've spent almost all my life alone. I don't know how to behave with others. I could never figure out what to say to her. I'd make a fool of myself. I'd just stand there, my courtship gift hanging from my talon. My beak open, flies buzzing in and out. I'd feel much better if you'd do it." He peeled off a strip of meat with one talon and leaned over to place it in his open beak. "I saw her approach the humans."

Kyp shook his head admiringly. "*That* was gutsy."

"Yes." Kuper pulled up a short strip, tossed it in the air and quickly swallowed it. "And stupid."

"She says she's seen humans repeat some of our words. *Our* words. As many as sixteen. Can you believe that?"

"Oh, I can believe it. Why not? Humans look hopeless, but they're clever. They've found ways to swim and dig. Even ways to fly. There isn't much they can't do." He ripped off another short strip of meat and swallowed it. "But the Old Ones are right about one thing — humans can't be trusted."

"You worry too much about the humans."

"*You* don't worry enough. And I mean that." Kuper took an uncharacteristically serious tone. "Never, *never* trust the human, or anything to do with the human. Do you hear me?" He stared intently at Kyp, then returned to his meal. "I'm telling you this for your own good. If you repeat that one phrase over and over, you might remember it and survive. Say it to yourself every night before you sleep." He tore another strip off the carcass. "I do."

Kuper pecked at his food in silence, then continued. "My nest-family and cousins to the nest made that mistake. They trusted the human. All of us roosted in a grove of old oak next to a long field of corn. We returned every year, at least that was what I was told. I was only a newling. Plenty of corn for everyone, human and Crow. There were only, maybe, eight humans roosted near that field, and the corn went on — I was young, maybe I just remember it this way — it seemed like the corn went on *forever*. To the horizon. Beyond the horizon. I was young, so I stayed out when the sun was setting, testing my wings. I'd fly until I was tired, then land in the field and eat. Fly and eat, fly and eat. For a newling, it was the perfect existence.

"One evening, just after the final sixth, everyone had roosted except me. Apart from the mosquitoes and frogs, it was dead quiet. Then, suddenly, I heard this thunder. I glanced up to check how far away it was and instead saw this

— I don't know how to describe it — this … vision. See, it wasn't thunder, or if it was, it was thunder that had crept right down to the ground, because there were flashes of light erupting from among the trees. The trees weren't hurt by this lightning — weren't shattered, weren't burned, weren't blasted — but my cousins, my father, my mother, my sisters, they were all falling. Dropping like ripe fruit.

"And then I saw *them*. Humans. Crouching. On their bellies. Hidden among the bushes. Smoke emerging from the tips of their stingers. And each time the smoke billowed, thunder followed, and another Crow dropped. The humans had slithered through the reeds, silent as fog. I flew toward the trees. I called and I called, but the thunder continued and my Family kept tumbling.

"My great-grandfather caught me and ordered me to hide in the tall reeds by a nearby stream. We lay in the thick, sticky mud by the roots, listening to that *bang, bang, bang*, from one stinger and then another, like a horrible echo, and the wavering cries of my Family. Calling out warning. Calling out in pain. Crying for help.

"It was like a long, painful nightmare. Eventually it stopped and everything became quiet again — even inside my head. We lay there in the muck. I don't know how long. It seemed like forever.

"I had wanted so badly to do something to stop them, but what could I have done? I've considered that many times. What could I have done?" Kuper ripped a great strip off the carcass with a jerk of his thick neck, then let the meat drop.

"My grandfather had received a great ragged gash down his throat. He wheezed and bled into the mud all night, then died while I slept. When I woke, his spirit had joined the Maker and I was completely alone in the world. He was the last of my line. My entire nest-family from the branch out was lost that night, every one to the human. I flew in and out of the oak trees where I'd last seen them. Searching. All that remained were feathers and dried blood. The humans had scavenged everything else — bodies, bones and beaks.

"I felt discarded. A leftover. I was nothing to anything anymore. I let the wind take me that day. It's blown me across oceans, to lands I don't even know the names of. I've flown wherever the wind directed, and I can tell you this: everything in life eats something, but humans would eat the world if they could. They'll be hungry until they have crushed and swallowed every tree, every seed, every blade of grass, every bird, insect and animal. And I'll tell you something else, something I learned that night, something the wind whispered to me as I flew away: there's nothing to be gained by hiding. I'll never hide from anything again."

Kuper placed the carcass at Kyp's talons. "Give this to Kym when she returns. Ask if she'll accept it. If she will, tell her I'm interested in making a match."

143

"Don't you think you should talk to her first?"

"Just ask her," Kuper called over his shoulder as he leaped from the branch, then flew off, those big black wings seizing the air in powerful, slow strokes. Solitary, as usual.

The clouds rolled in that afternoon. The rains started shortly after.

CHAPTER 16

When you are a newling, you know the wind only as the Wind. Once you grow older, you understand that things are more complicated. The wind can be a friend. The wind can be a parent. The wind can be an enemy. When the wind is a friend, you play with it. When the wind is a parent, you learn from it. When the wind is your enemy, you hide.

Clouds skidded swiftly across the sky — low, heavy and dark. Kyp huddled in a bushy spruce by the shores of the beaver pond and tried to keep warm. Other creatures found shelter according to their abilities — the beaver in his den, the mouse in her burrow. Here and there, a Crow perched in a field and pecked at worms as they rose to the surface, but mostly we nestled in our trees, close to the trunk, heads tucked into our shoulders, the rain running in streams off our backs and tail feathers.

The storm blew long into the afternoon, and under its force the Gathering Tree bent and shivered. Then, abruptly, it shifted to the north and picked up. All through the tree, one could sense Crow heads turning and listening, wondering.

Shortly after sunset, the rain turned to snow. Within a brief time, it swirled about in vast, impenetrable white sheets. As dusk fell, it began to accumulate on the ground, and by midnight, the snow was piled Crow high on every branch.

Spring is the worst time for a blizzard. Midwinter snows fall cold, dry and light — each flake gossamer dropped from a chick. In the spring, clouds arrive heavy with moisture and the snows fall fat and sticky. Leaves have emerged, so each tree retains the snow's full weight. Now, as the snow gathered, you could hear trees groan and strain under the heft of this wet, weighty mass.

The temperature dropped — and then dropped again. Cold can best be measured by the discomfort it causes. This cold hurt to breathe. Wing tips burned as if touched by flame. We huddled together in the dark, each Crow clinging with numb talons to the branch as the wind pelted snow.

By this time, we all knew the storm was a serious affair

— I couldn't recall anything that had arrived with such speed or fury. I kept turning over in my mind where we might find better shelter, but the dark and the snow had come too quickly. We Crows pride ourselves on our ability to laugh our way through trouble. Storytelling is the way we're most likely to pass a cold evening together. It's one small indication of how anxious we all were that up and down the tree you could hear the wind gnawing branches and limbs, but not a single story being told.

Kym shivered on the branch next to me, looking grimly out at the bleak, swirling landscape. Finally she said, "You know what?"

"What, Niece?"

"I hate snow. What's to like? It's cold, it's wet — I know the Maker has her reasons, but isn't it possible that even she made a bit of an oversight? And night. Why create that? Dark. Cold. A lot of scary ... black. I mean, it'd be nice, don't you think, if we were a different color? Something that would break the darkness, rather than add to it."

I had to laugh. In that moment, as I considered Kym's glum expression, I realized just how much she reminded me of my wife in her younger days. Karla had never approved of winter or snow or the cold, either, and had always been happiest when we roosted along the coast down south. "Oh, Kymmy," I said and shook my tail to remove some snow. "I can't agree. What could be more beautiful than a shining coat of black feathers? What could be more elegant than black?" I asked. "Everything mysterious and beautiful in the world is black. The rich, dark soil, host to all manner of delicious bugs and plants. The center of the eye, where the soul resides. Ideas, before they become ideas, form in the warm black ferment of your imagination." I blinked and looked out at the storm raging beyond the protection of the branches. "Your hummingbirds are beautiful, I'll give you that, and yellow finches can look like stars fallen to Earth, but black is a color the Maker loves to use, Niece. She used it for us and she used it for the beginning of everything back before First Time."

Kym rearranged herself to shed some snow from her tail. "You almost make it sound nice, Uncle. But I still can't find my way to like it."

So we crouched there in the darkness, all of us together — the tree quaking, the snow pelting down, half frozen, half wind-blown — and stared bleakly at the storm. After one particularly strong gust of wind shivered the tree, Kymmy said in her quiet voice, "Tell me about the beginning of things, Uncle."

I shifted and drew my wings in tighter. "Ah. The beginning of things. Before either sun or Earth or star, there was the black night sky and it stretched from beginning to end. At the very center of the darkness sat the Maker, and she was lonely. So she sang and shaped us from the darkness, from the air and from her dreams. And that is how Great Crow was born. Together, Great Crow and the Maker soared across that vast emptiness, sometimes the Maker first, sometimes Great Crow. They swooped and tumbled without fear, and the Maker laughed. That was the Hanana — the First Laugh — and its vibrations are with us still. When you fly and suddenly feel happy for no reason at all, or nestle into the crook of a branch and the weariness drops from you like rainwater from a feather, it is said that you have been touched by the echoes of the Hanana.

"After a time, the Maker and Great Crow grew tired and needed a place to roost, and so the Maker sang again. She sang stars to guide her and light to see by, and then sang the First Nest, and that nest was the Earth. And, in time, she laid an enormous brood of eggs, and those eggs hatched to become every other living thing on Earth. So everything has its reason to be proud, for we're all descended from the Maker, but before anything else, there was Great Crow. We were the Maker's first companion."

The branch swayed under the weight of a bird landing. I looked up and saw Kyp, trying to maintain a grip on the branch, shaking snow from his head.

"What are you doing here?" I whispered. "You are *forbidden* to return."

"I just —"

"*Forbidden*, do you understand?" I glanced about to see if

anyone else had noticed him. "You could be Banished, your name stricken from the Family records. Disobedience of a direct ruling is unforgivable. Now go. Find cover as best you can. Search for shelter in a cliffside, do whatever — but don't return to the Family for help until —"

"I *didn't* come back for help," he said. "I came back to guide the Family to a safe roost."

That stopped me quick. "What are you talking about?"

Suddenly, the branch dipped again and two other figures perched. Kyrk and Ketch, bristling from the quill out, doubling their size. Had it not been dark and every Crow focused on trying to survive the storm and cold, just the sight of them would have caused a Mob to gather.

"What's *he* doing here?" Ketch barked over the roar of the wind.

"Who gave *him* permission to return?" growled Kyrk.

I nodded at Kyp. "He says he's come back to help."

"Help with *what?* I'll show him help!" Ketch blustered. "This will be the last time he —"

I cut him off. "He says he knows a place where the Family can get out of the storm."

"Nonsense!" Kyrk snorted. "What roost can he possibly have found that we haven't seen many times during past Gatherings?"

"Collect the Family for a judgment," Ketch commanded.

"Don't be an idiot," Kyrk said witheringly. "We're in the

middle of a storm."

And as if it was reminded of its presence, the wind suddenly seized the tree. Each limb thrashed dizzyingly. Above, a branch shuddered and split with an explosive crack. A flurry of snow, leaves and bark tumbled down, and the Crows perched on it rose into the air, squawking in terror.

Ignoring the others, Kyp spoke directly to me. "We have to go, and we have to go now."

Kyrk glowered at Kyp, then turned to me. "What's his plan?"

"As far as I can tell," Ketch interrupted, "there *is* only one plan. And my bet is," and he swung his head at Kyp, "that he's just come back to benefit from it."

That caught me off guard. What was he talking about? "And what plan might that be?"

"Stay put. Wait out the storm. If it gets worse, invoke Cluster."

"Cluster?" Kyp repeated. "You're not serious?"

Cluster Rules are invoked in the worst emergency conditions only. The Flock clusters and relies on the warmth provided by the bodies to generate heat. When one goes to Cluster, one as much as acknowledges that not everyone will survive. I had been avoiding invoking Cluster, praying that the storm would abate.

"We can't go to Cluster, Uncle," Kyp interrupted. "You

can protect your younger ones a short while by shifting them to the center, but what about your elders? How long will they last on the perimeter? If this storm keeps building, going to Cluster will condemn most of the flock. *We have to leave.*"

"*And go where?*" Under the pressure of the storm, I felt my patience running thin. "Do you think I haven't been asking myself that? I've been reviewing all my past trips, all the past Gatherings, and as far as I can remember, there's no better shelter for the Kinaar within a day's flight."

Kyp hesitated a moment and then said, "I know a place."

"How could you *possibly* know of a place that we haven't already seen?" Kyrk said, dismissing the idea with a flap of his wing.

Kyp looked first to me, then at Kyrk. "Because it's underground."

The idea was so outrageous that Kyrk and Ketch seemed not to even understand what Kyp was talking about. Then Kyrk squinted at Kyp, shook himself completely to remove the snow gathering on his back and barked, "Underground? You mean, *down* underground?" Kyp nodded. "Are you out of your mind?"

"It's forbidden," Ketch snapped. "Crows can't survive *underground.*"

"It's a wide roost, and relatively dry and —"

"Doesn't matter how wide it is, doesn't matter how dry,"

Ketch interrupted. "It's not *allowed* and it's not *safe*. How can you tell what kind of creatures are hiding down there?"

"It *is* safe. Safer than here," Kyp said and looked about at the Crows huddled near the trunk. "And warmer."

"How can you be sure?" Ketch asked.

"Because I've *been* there. I know."

That stopped everyone in mid-flap. Kyrk recovered first.

"Ridiculous!" he snorted. "He hasn't gone underground. Even *he* wouldn't break the commandments when he's already in disgrace."

"I was there," Kyp persisted. "I saw the place. I know it's forbidden —"

"You *knew* it was forbidden —," Ketch sputtered.

"— but it's perfect," Kyp continued. "It's sheltered, it's warm, it's large enough to accommodate everyone. And we don't have a choice. In a few moments, we'll have lost our opportunity. Some of the older ones and most of the younger ones won't be able to move. This place is out of the wind and snow, and there's a hot spring that seeps in." Another branch snapped, sending Crows tumbling. "*Look at what's happening.* We have to *do* something."

A wheezing cough rattled behind me. I turned and saw Kork, every cord of his stringy frame straining against the wind, edging over on the branch.

"I've heard you talking," he said and coughed once again. "And for once I agree with the youngster. We have to do something." He peered into the night and sniffed the breeze. "This is a great-grandfather storm. It's wicked now, and still drawing power. We haven't seen its worst." He glanced out at the rest of the flock. Some of the young were struggling to stay upright. "We stay here, perform Cluster, at least half the Family will meet the Maker." Then he looked back at Kyp. "But me and mine won't go underground."

"But it's —" Kyp interrupted.

"Doesn't matter. No point talking about it. Waste of everyone's breath. It's forbidden — end of story. Even if it wasn't forbidden, none of my Clan would set talon or claw in a place dug out by an undergrounder. The Kemna have never gone underground. We're not about to start. But there's a tall, narrow human roost south and east of here. Empty in its upper reaches. Big crisscrossing piece of wood, like a perch set up top. Couple of large clanging things up there that humans like to shake. Make a tremendous noise. If we were looking for a place out of the wind for some of the Family, it might do."

I vaguely recollected the roost. Pigeons made themselves comfortable there. It was within flying distance, barely. "I think I know the place you're talking about."

I tried to recall the shelter's exact size. "But how much room has it?"

"Not near enough for everyone. A hundred maybe — the Kemna and a few dozen more. It'd be tight, but tight is good under the circumstances."

"It would mean splitting the flock."

Kork squinted at me and gave a nod of acknowledgment. "I'd choose for my bunch. The rest of you would have to fly with —" He indicated Kyp with the slightest dismissive nod. "— this one. But whatever you decide, do it now. I won't take them unless you say. I'm content to form Cluster, take our chances, if you give the word. Maybe means we lose a good portion of the Kinaar — so be it, if that's what the night brings. But me and mine won't break our bond with the Maker."

Snow gathered on the lids and in the corners of our eyes. I blinked and tried to clear my mind. Whichever way I went, the choices seemed equally bad.

Kyrk leaned in close and muttered, "If we don't do something soon, there won't be a Family to split." He shook his head impatiently to scatter the snow that had gathered there. Immediately snow clung to his head and back again.

I was thinking as fast as I could. If the Family separated now, there might be no coming back together again. There were already too many conflicts dug in under the skin. This would be the grounds for a more formal Splitting. If we survived, some would claim it was a choice between maintaining or breaking the ancient laws. So I could keep the Kinaar together at the Gathering Tree and condemn them, or I could give permission to a Splitting, which could potentially divide us forever. How could I keep the Family together only to condemn them to a slow death? How could I split our Family and face my ancestors when the storm ended?

"All right," I said at last, "it's decided. The Kinaar will fly in two groups. One following Kork. The other, Kyp."

Kyrk understood the implications of the decision better than the others. "You're sure?" he asked.

"Yes."

"And who will you fly with, Uncle?" Kyp asked.

"Here's how we'll do it," I started. "I'll fly with Kork, make sure they arrive safely —"

"But, Uncle —," Kyp objected.

"*Then*," I continued, "I'll come join you."

Kyrk shot me a sharp look. "Ridiculous!"

"Two flights?" Kyp protested. "In this weather? It's impossible to make the journey there and back."

"For once, he's right," Kyrk agreed. "It's impossible."

"*I'm* the Chooser," I said loudly. "I have a responsibility to the Family. To *all* the Family. Kyrk, you will follow Kyp and act as backup."

"Me?" Kyrk glowered. "Provide backup for *him*?"

"Yes, you," I snapped. "To fulfill your obligation to the Family, of course — not for Kyp."

"Do you take me for a fledgling?" he bristled, glaring.

I stood to my full height. "No, sir, I take you for an *elder*, one of our most respected elders, one who understands the responsibilities of his position. Do you refuse?"

Kyrk hesitated a few moments before answering. "No. I understand," he replied slowly. "I'll do as you ask."

"Good," I said and released a sigh. "Then go, all of you. Organize the move."

May the Maker help me, it was the only solution I could think of. If I could serve as a link between these groups, then maybe when this was over, there might be a way to mend things.

"Spread the word!" I shouted, trying to be heard over the sound of another branch cracking. "Organize the Clans. We will move as quickly as possible."

Kyrk looked out at the storm, up at the Family and finally at Kyp. "Wait," he said. "Listen a moment. Tell them they're being taken somewhere safe. Tell them to get ready. But don't say a word about roosting underground."

"But —," Kyp began.

"Don't," Kyrk repeated. "Once they've arrived, they'll go in, even if it takes some persuasion. But if you tell them everything now, you'll never convince the older ones."

Kyp looked to me, and I indicated my agreement with a nod. "Fair enough," he said.

"Give me directions and I'll find my way there," I told him. "I have to see Kork and his Clan off first."

"Why, Uncle?"

"Because I'm the Chooser," I sighed, "and whatever happens, it's up to me to see that everyone arrives safely."

Kyp shook some snow off his beak and looked at me. I could see concern behind his eyes.

"Don't worry, Nephew," I assured him. "I'll find my way."

The word traveled through the tree, Crow to Crow, beak to beak. The Family divided into their Clans. Guards, sentries and outposts were appointed to each unit.

It was the first time that the Kinaar had undergone a Splitting. It was the first time in my remembrance that the Kinaar had been forced to abandon the security of the Gathering Tree. Knowing this almost broke my heart. At last Kym slipped onto the branch next to me.

"Uncle, I've been asked to tell you that everyone is ready," she murmured softly.

"That's fine. I'm just receiving some final directions from Kyp here."

Kym moved closer to Kyp. "Kork will lead the Kemnas and I understand that you will guide the rest of the Family to the tunnel."

"That's right," Kyp said.

"So," she said and nudged him a little, "it looks as if your explorations were of some use after all."

"It looks that way," he replied, ducking his head.

She fixed him with a steady gaze. "You think it's safe,

Kyp? Truly?"

Kyp let his gaze move to the chaos swirling just beyond the tree limb. "Tonight, it's safer than this roost. Of that, I'm certain."

"I wish I was going with you. I'm sure you think you know what you're doing, but —" She sighed and gave a small shake of her head. "— I'm just as certain you could benefit from my advice."

Kyp dipped his head once again. "You know you're more than welcome to come," he murmured.

"I understand, but my place is with my Clan." Kym turned to me again. "Can I ask you to reconsider, Uncle? Please? I'm afraid for you. Stay with us. Appoint someone else to take temporary responsibility for the others. I would gladly go back to check on things if you would allow it."

I shook my head. "I can't do that. It is *my* responsibility. My place is with *all* my Family."

Kym sighed again. "If that's your final decision, I've been sent to tell you that the Kinaar are ready."

"Thank you," I said and quietly began the Traveler's Blessing. "Fly straight," I said and heard both Kyp and Kym join me. "Roost safely. Let the Maker guide us to a safe perch."

Kym leaned against Kyp a moment. "I'll see you when the storm breaks," she said, then raised her wings. "Take care, Kyp. The wind under your wings, and may the Maker protect you."

"And you," Kyp replied. "And Good eating at the other end."

With that, nearly a thousand pairs of wings stirred and we began our journey into the night — and the teeth of the storm.

CHAPTER 17

And so the Splitting I'd avoided for so long arrived. Just over a hundred and sixty head flew after Kork; the remainder took wing with Kyp. The best thing that could be said of the Splitting was that I had managed to keep Kyrk among the majority. Had he flown with Kork, I'm certain at least two other Clans would have elected to join him, and I'm not sure how many would have followed Kyp.

But even with Kyrk assisting, organizing this passage was a challenge in those stormy conditions. Fliers were sent out to collect those who were away from the tree and to communicate with those on the tree. Mothers collected chicks. Clan leaders sent word down. Families with close connections in the separating Clans had to decide who they would travel with. Voices grew clamorous as brothers and sisters took leave of one another under the worst possible conditions. Newlings wept as they realized favorite aunts and uncles wouldn't accompany them.

At last everything was made ready, and Kyp slipped into the wind and was swallowed whole by the darkness, more than eight hundred souls trailing behind him. Although spotters and wing ends were appointed, keeping formation was incredibly difficult. But without order, there was no way that eight hundred and some Crows would arrive at the same place through that wind and snow.

The organization of Crows is elegant in a way one doesn't find among other birds. When geese lumber into the wind, you can see the rigid organization. When Crows fly, the structure is invisible. We have had eternity to make it work, even with the large numbers we travel with, even in a crisis such as this. How many times have you seen geese lost in a fog, calling to one another? This would be unthinkable for a Crow.

I'll say it again — even in terrible times, when a Crow flies, he flies with style.

CHAPTER 18

From the moment of our departure from the Gathering Tree — one portion of the Family moving in one direction and the other in another, the storm raging all around — you may have assumed that no one noticed. This would be incorrect.

As we abandoned our roost, at least one creature paid very close attention. From some safe place deep within the shadows, one creature studied us carefully with curiosity, hunger and a deep, brooding anger.

Perhaps he had hoped that the storm would force us to the ground. Perhaps he simply assumed that the storm and cold would bring death, and so deliver him food. Perhaps he had been watching us since his public humiliation, waiting for the right moment to exact his revenge. No one can be certain.

But we can assume this. The Red watched us, noticed that the larger portion of the flock moved down the valley and followed. When he discovered where the flock was roosting for the night, he thought, planned and returned to his home. Not directly, however.

All members of the Cat Family are solitary creatures. Large or small, they hunt and live alone. And this is true even of cats that are slaves of humans. But as they differ in many of their habits from their wilder cousins, so do they differ in this: on rare occasions, they will gather and work as a group.

The Red almost always hunted alone. There were times, however, when he would team up with one of several others who lived in the vicinity. Some say they were all descendants of the Red, although they shared no particular resemblance, except in wickedness. But if wickedness was dependent upon lineage only, there'd be much less of it in this world than there is.

Four other cats, all younger than the Red, were known to Crows through previous unwelcome contact. The first, a great shaggy white snowball of a cat, with gray-green eyes and an enormous appetite for birds. A ring with a noisemaker that jingle-jangled had been fashioned by his human master and fastened around his neck — some said as a reward for killing so many birds. Next came a tan short-haired cat with long legs, a lithe, sinewy body and a tail that never stopped twitching. A muscular, compact black-and-orange-striped cat was the third of this murderous crew, his eyes a penetrating gray blue. The last of this foul bunch was one as black as the snowball was white and silent as shade when it stalked. Although none held the same reputation as the Red, all were notorious in their own fashion. The White especially could be counted on to toy with his prey.

I later learned all this from a jay who spent the evening crouched in its nest near our Gathering Tree and saw the procession: When the Red left that night and stalked into the storm — ears back, belly down — four other cats followed: one striped, one tan, one snow white and one dark as a smudge of smoke trailing behind.

CHAPTER 19

Kork labored through the blizzard and behind him flew his Clan. Flying backup were Kuper and Kym on left wing, I on right. My thoughts as we cut through the night I will not share. They were uniformly dark.

Buffeted by wind, frozen, unable to see, we endured a hard flight and, for so short a distance, a long, long one. It was not only the physical trial of the journey that made it difficult; a tremendous uneasiness ran through the flock and weakened every stroke of every wing.

As we flew, Kuper, who had always been so silent, proved himself useful in a hundred ways. Now he came alongside a yearling struggling against the wind and shouted words of encouragement. Now he flew parallel to an elder straying off course and gently nudged him back into formation. Everyone understood that once you were lost in this storm, you were lost forever. There could be no going back to find someone.

And so we flew, each Crow struggling for breath, tired and cold and spent. At last Kork saw the dark outline of a tall human structure. He called to the others, banked left and swept up — we had come in low, trying to avoid the powerful wind currents that range above trees and the tops of human roosts.

Up we circled and at last Kork landed. Each Crow awaited the Call to Roost, but none came back. We hovered, rocked by the wind, wings tired, waiting. Kuper swooped in alongside Kym. "What's happening?" he panted. "Why doesn't he call us in? Some of the older ones can't fly much longer."

"Can't you see?" Kym turned to him. "There's no place to go. The entrance to the roost has been covered."

So began a nightmare for all the Family who had followed Kork. The cold, already so fierce that ice crystals formed round each Crow's eyes, was made ten times worse by the relentless wind. A narrow ledge we had discovered produced some small protection. It was in the lee of the wind, but gusts and buffets curled and looped from all sides. Kym clung to it, and it was only with great difficulty that Kuper landed and crept along beside her.

"Are there *any* openings?" she shouted.

"None," Kuper called back. "I've circled all round. Nothing."

I scratched at the wood panels with a claw. "Is there a portion we could pull apart? Any place we could peck through?"

Kuper shook his head. "Useless. I've tried. The wood's too thick. Our folk are throwing themselves at it and all they're doing is hurting themselves."

Kym scanned the massive structure. "Why would the humans close it up tonight?"

"It makes no sense!" Kuper shouted bitterly. "Which means for humans it makes perfect sense."

"We can't stay here!" Kym yelled.

Kuper shook snow from the end of his beak. "Where else can we go?"

"I don't know," she answered dully, and then lowered her voice and glanced at me. "Uncle Kork won't move us again. Coming here took it all out of him."

"Same for everyone." Kuper gestured with a wing to the other figures clinging to the ledge off in the darkness, just barely holding on. "Look at them. They're in no shape to move. There's nothing to do now but take Cluster."

I nodded. "But where? Where can we Cluster where we have any hope of getting through the night?"

Suddenly Kurt, a small Crow, fluttered down beside us.

"Kalum!" he called. "You better come. It's Kork."

I struggled to be heard above the wind. "What about him?"

"He fell!"

Kym, Kuper and I launched from the ledge and flung ourselves back into the wind.

"Where is he?" I shouted.

"Down there," Kurt called and dipped his head.

We circled briefly, then dropped to the ground. Already, drifting snow was beginning to cover the limp body.

"Uncle?" Kym stepped close and nudged his body. Kork didn't move. "Uncle?" she repeated and placed her beak close to his. Again, nothing.

"How did this happen?" she asked Kurt.

"Nobody knows. One minute he was with the rest, then he was gone. The wind might have thrown him."

Kym crouched closer to the body on the ground. "Uncle?" she whispered. "Uncle, get up."

She brushed the snow from his face and nuzzled his beak. The wiry black body that had led his Clan for so long lay unmoving, suddenly frail and small.

I stepped in beside Kym. "Leave him, Niece. This night he's made his trip."

We gently tucked Kork's head under one wing. I delivered a brief prayer, then stamped the snow from my talons. Kork was complicated and difficult to understand, yet no one worked harder for his Family. What is death but a short flight to a better roost? He'd more than earned his rest.

Looking down at that old fellow, now just a shell, I suddenly felt bitterly tired and incompetent. Fortunately Kuper shook me from my reverie. He knocked the snow from his beak and nodded out at the swirling darkness. "Shall we try to find Kyp?"

Kym shook her head. "It's too far. We've all been exposed to the wind too long." She nodded at the line of yearlings crouched nearby. "They'd never make it."

"I say we return to the Gathering Tree then," Kuper said and impatiently shook snow off his beak again. "This shelter is worse than nothing. At least at the Gathering Tree there's some slight protection and we'll have a better chance if we go to Cluster."

"It's so far," I pointed out. "And so soon after flying here. How many are up to it?"

I tried to collect my thoughts, but Kym suddenly looked up and said cautiously, "I have an idea."

At that moment, a yearling collapsed right beside us. Kym fluttered to her side.

"Katy?" she asked. "What's the matter?"

"I can't feel anything, Kymmy," the yearling whispered. "My wings won't work anymore."

One of the spotters hovered near us, then dropped

beside Kuper. After a few moments of hurried conversation, Kuper slid in beside Kym.

"We've lost eight more on the far side of the ledge," he said. "This fellow, Kelk, says there are some on the windward side that have simply put to ground and are letting the snow cover them. We won't survive the night here," he said matter-of-factly. "Not one of us."

"Where else can we go?" I snapped. "The wind's picked up. Branches, even thick ones, are being snapped and tossed about. There's no shelter nearby and we can't fly any distance to do a proper search. If we go back to the Gathering Tree, we'll lose half this bunch just in the flight."

Kym looked down at little Katy. "I know where," she said.

"What?" Kuper asked.

"I know a place," she said in a louder voice. "It's not far."

"Where?" I asked.

"How far is not far?" Kuper added, squinting at the storm.

Kym first glanced at me, then at Kuper. "It's a gamble. You'll have to trust me."

"At this point," I said, "I'm willing to try almost anything."

Kym crouched near the small Crow and bent her head so that her voice could be heard above the clamor of the wind. "Katy, you have to get up."

The smaller bird shook her head. "I can't."

"You have to. We're going somewhere more sheltered. It'll be better there."

"I can't even feel my shoulders anymore," Katy said in a quiet, sleepy voice. "I'll just rest here a little while."

Kuper bent his head down. "Can you crawl onto my back?"

Kym looked up at him sharply. "You can't carry her."

Kuper crouched low in the snow and spread his wings. "I'll be fine," he said shortly and stooped.

"You'll never be able to fly with her on your back," Kym protested. "Not in this weather. Katy, you'll have to —"

Kuper interrupted her. "Shh. It's all right. She weighs less than some of the scavenge I've fetched to a cache." Then he urged Katy once more in a gentle voice. "Can you stand?"

"I think so," the youngster answered.

She rose slowly, first to her haunches and then to her talons. Crawling softly onto Kuper's back, she sighed and settled in. I was taken aback at the size difference. She appeared so tiny nestled into the feathers on Kuper's broad back.

Kuper eased to a standing position. "Hold tight," he warned the youngster. "And keep your beak flattened against the nape of my neck."

"You'll both be knocked to the ground by the first strong gust," Kym warned, shaking her head.

Kuper looked at Kym. "Now. Where to?"

"Follow me," she called, launching herself into the storm.

The Call spread from one to another that we were to move again. The Kemna reacted with equal measures of hope and despair. Hope, because everyone understood that we'd not survive the night here; despair, because we were already exhausted, and forging out once more into the snow and wind was more than some could bear. In the deepening drifts by the base of the human's roost, we left nearly forty bodies who would never fly or laugh or see Family again in this world. Of all the losses we took that night, I regret these most bitterly, a result solely of my poor judgment and bad choosing.

Kym circled and called to the gathering flock, "Everyone! Stay within sight of someone. If you can't see tail feathers ahead of you, you're too far behind. Keep your eyes open for treetops — I'll be flying low."

With that, she dipped her wings and swooped south.

Kuper followed closely behind her. "If I'm to fly rear guard," he called to her, "I've got to know where you're taking us."

"To the humans," Kym replied.

CHAPTER 20

In the meantime, eight hundred and some Crows struggled through the dark, led by Kyp and prodded by Kyrk, who was relentless in his urging. Pity the Crows who lagged that night — Kyrk found them and nipped their legs. Sympathize with the poor souls who, driven by the wind, veered off course. Kyrk was there in an instant, with a hard blow of his wings, a harsh word and clear direction.

When a hungry brown owl suddenly appeared out of the gloom and flew alongside the right wing looking for stragglers, it was Kyrk who quickly enlisted ten others to discourage it. The owl disappeared as swiftly as the sun and grass and spring itself had disappeared earlier that day.

When at last, tired, beaten and gasping, the flock began

to drop to the ground, it was in large measure due to Kyrk's efforts that the group was still intact.

Kyp led them in a column through the driving snow, swooping low over the earth, dipping down a valley and finally stooping deep near the bottom of a ravine. He lowered his legs and landed in drifting snow.

As the others landed and spied the underground entrance, they began to shuffle about nervously. "What are we doing here?" they muttered.

"We'll roost in there for the night," Kyp called and tipped his head in the direction of the tunnel.

"Underground?" You could hear the word repeated up and down the flock. "Underground?" And each time the word was said again, one could sense deepening fear. Underground — the forbidden world, the home of badgers, burrowing owls, weasels and a thousand other deadly enemies.

Even with the cold and the storm, voices called belligerently, "We can't go there. We're not mice." Others whimpered, "There'll be snakes."

Kyp fluttered atop a fallen tree and turned to face the Family. He looked at all the faces staring desperately at him, bodies crowded together trying to keep warm, some attempting to peer down the tunnel, some already looking back into the storm for escape.

"I've been inside," Kyp called to the flock, and there

were further murmurs of shock. "There's a safe warm roost that will accommodate every one of us for the night. It will be all right if you'll just stay close and follow me." The worried muttering grew until Kyp shouted above it. "If we remain above ground, we'll all die!" The murmuring stopped as his blunt assessment struck home. "There is no other place. Now, who's with me? Kyrk?"

For a long moment, Kyrk didn't move. Then he stepped in close and muttered something.

"What?" Kyp asked, unable to understand.

"I can't," Kyrk repeated.

Kyp stepped back and stared. "What do you mean 'I can't'?"

"I mean, this is a foolish mistake," he whispered gruffly. "Great Crow, don't ask me to walk into a place where I can't even *see*. I won't willingly violate my relationship with the Maker, and I won't ask others to, either. Crows were never meant for, for *burrowing*."

"We don't have to burrow —"

"There's likely to be weasels in there, or worse."

As Kyrk was saying this, others were crowding around him, hopping over the snow, trying to find out what the difficulty was.

"It's empty, Uncle." Kyp tried to keep his voice calm. "How many times can I tell you —"

"How can you be certain?" Kyrk objected. "How?"

"I've checked," Kyp replied as matter-of-factly as he could, trying to keep the conversation private.

"We can stay here. We can shelter from the wind at the mouth of the cave. We don't actually have to go in."

"The flock won't survive here. Half of them are on their last wing now. They need warmth. They need to get out of the wind. The only place they can get that is in there."

Kyrk stubbornly shook his head. "I won't do it."

Kyp moved even closer to the older Crow. "I know you don't trust me, but ... You can't survive the night out here, Uncle."

Kyrk snorted. "You think I haven't weathered storms before?"

Kyp leaned in close. "*Why?* Why won't you come?"

Kyrk didn't reply, but as they stared at each other, beak to beak, Kyp suddenly understood. He realized that this old Crow who had faced owl and marten in his time was paralyzed with fear.

Kyp felt the pressure of the flock hanging on his decision. He dropped his voice so only Kyrk could hear. "Then take rear guard, Uncle. Stand at the entrance. Keep watch. But don't discourage the others from going in. *Please.*"

The older bird stared levelly at the younger, then Kyrk abruptly turned to the rest of the flock.

"Well?" he shouted. "What are you waiting for? *Get in!*

The sooner you're in, the sooner you'll be out of the wind. Go on. I'm behind you."

Several of Kyp's younger comrades needed no further urging. They surged forward, and that made all the difference. At once, others began crowding in, and soon Kyp was leading the flock, step by step, into the tunnel's tight confines.

Subdued and weary, the Family filed silently through the dark. The last Crow had only barely entered the tunnel when an eerie moan rose to a shrill, tormented wail that echoed up and down the tunnel. The feathers of each Crow stood erect. "The spirits of our ancestors," some muttered. "The Maker's warning."

Kyp raised his voice over the noise. "It's only the wind!"

Slowly, the Family trudged on, but the voiceless whispers, howls and moans trailed after them. Each Crow proceeded carefully, trusting the individual in front not to stumble or fall. The smell of fear and wet Crow filled the shaft. What little there was of light came slanting through the holes the humans had cut in the ceiling. Through accident, planning or some effect of the weather, the humans' lights above the tunnel flickered. They flared, dimmed, crackled and moments later popped and flared again.

It was by these erratic bursts and flashes that one Crow followed another into the deepening gloom.

CHAPTER 21

The Kemnas — weary to the bone — sought to keep up with Kym. "To the humans," she'd said. But what did that mean? The notion was so unbelievable there scarcely seemed any point in discussing it. Nor was there any energy for discussion. We flew. We flew because we knew there was no other option.

It was the worst flight of my life. Not knowing what had happened to the other part of the Family or if they had found safe refuge. Leaving Kork and the other unfortunates to be covered by the snow and flying to a roost even more uncertain than the one we were leaving. I tried to concentrate on my flight. The wind had grown in intensity, howling and clawing, each new gust battering the body and numbing the spirit. Flight became erratic, staying on course almost impossible. Kymmy had wisely selected a route that wasn't directly against the wind, but that kept the wind for the most part on our right. That meant, however, that for every stroke of a wing, she had to take another to correct her course. Finally, she folded her wings and landed in a bent, battered crab apple tree just beyond a small rectangular human roost.

Several branches were splintered, a number were snapped outright. The topmost twigs spun crazily, attached to the tree's body by only the thinnest bits and strips of bark. The flock dropped wearily onto the crab apple or into the branches of a nearby birch. Kym hopped onto a ledge that projected from the human roost. Light spilled out of the roost, and against this warm glow, Kym appeared as a darkened silhouette.

"What are you doing?" Kuper hissed from a nearby branch.

"Just wait," she said, and though her voice was calm and controlled, she hesitated before tapping against the sheet of transparent stone that humans place over the holes in their roosts.

Alarmed, some of the Family raised their wings to fly. Most simply crouched in place, too dispirited to care, or too frozen and frightened to move. All at once, an immense, shaggy human face appeared at the opening and squinted into the storm. At first, the human seemed to see nothing. Then its eyes locked on Kym.

Normally the appearance of a human would have scattered the flock, but everyone was so wind blasted they merely stared at this bizarre spectacle. Slowly the human stretched out a long hairy limb, placed it against the clear stone and slid it open a crack.

As the wind whistled through the gap, Kym opened her beak. To my surprise, a strange, complicated series of foreign sounds emerged — not proper Crow words at all — but the incomprehensible mewlings, grunts, clicks and squeals of human communication. The human's eyes widened and it crouched forward. Kymmy repeated the eerie sounds.

Suddenly the human straightened, tilted its head and barked something. As if answering a summons, another human growled and scampered over. Both pressed their broad, fleshy faces close to the invisible stone barrier and studied Kym. Again Kym repeated her sounds, this time with what I took to be increased urgency.

The sounds appeared to register some powerful effect on the humans. They snorted, whistled and whooped back and forth at each other, making a terrible racket, all the while shooting wild glances at the sad, disheartened flock of Crows clinging to the trees beyond their roost. Us.

Finally, the larger, hairier one moved away from the invisible barrier and disappeared. Moments later, it reappeared at the ground level entrance to the roost, huddled beneath a thick layer of skins. It stalked determinedly through the deep snow. What had Kym done to make this strange creature abandon the warmth of its shelter and join us in the blizzard? It waded through the drifts, head down, until it arrived at a smaller roost. There, it pushed on a flat wooden barrier, which swung in. Having created an opening in this smaller roost, the human stood aside. Kym hopped off the ledge and, to my astonishment, swooped down to the opening. She hesitated at the threshold and then disappeared inside. Moments later, she returned and gave the Call to Roost.

Of course, no one moved a feather. What she was asking us to do defied all tradition, law and common sense. If we entered, had we any hope of ever leaving?

If I had been even a little less tired and my mind working better, I'm not sure what I would have done — joined her that much more quickly or turned at once and fled. But I was exhausted, as were all the others, and at last I shed my misgivings. I realized I would simply have to trust. Trust Kymmy, and trust the relationship she had somehow fostered with these humans. I fluttered down. Standing by Kym's side, I summoned what little voice I had left and repeated the Call. One after another, the Family hopped from the surrounding trees and sailed through the opening into this dark, mysterious roost.

Inside, it was cramped, only barely large enough to accommodate us — but warm and dry and out of the wind. One hundred and twenty of the Family entered and perched on wood outcroppings that ran the length of the roost above, or stood on the ground below. Instantly the cold began to leave our limbs. The last to approach was Kuper. He landed heavily on the snow outside the opening and crouched to allow little Katy to slip from his back. She fell, found her legs and limped into the shelter. Kuper hesitated at the entrance, then turned and leaped back into the air.

"Kuper!" Kym shouted to him. "What are you doing? Come in. It's safe."

He hunched his head, and I could see the strain on his face. "I can't!" he shouted back. "I can't go in."

Kym flew back toward the opening. "You *have* to, Kuper," she called, each word ripped from her beak and tossed into the wind. "There's nowhere else to go."

"I can't do it. I can't share a roost with the humans. I hate them."

A sudden gust of wind caught Kuper, and he fought to recover.

"Where will you go?" Kym shouted.

"What?" he asked as he struggled to maintain his position.

"Where. Will. You. Go?" She shouted each word separately to be heard above the storm.

"I'll find the others."

"How?"

"I know where Kyp was taking them."

"But will you make it? You're tired already."

"From here there's a way along the bottom of the coulee. It cuts out most of the wind. I'll be fine." Kym opened her beak to argue, but Kuper cut her short. "Kym," he blurted as another gust of wind caught him. "I should have spoken with you before. I should have …" He halted, then said so quietly it almost wasn't heard, "… a lot of things." Kuper had the habit of looking past you when he spoke, but for the first time, Kuper met Kym's eyes. "I'll talk to you when this storm has died," he said.

"Kuper," she said simply, "thank you. We couldn't have made it without you."

For a moment, Kuper's body straightened, and I thought in that instant he would change his mind. But he shifted a wing and swung into an updraft. "Good eating!" he called over his shoulder.

"Be careful," Kym called back as his form was erased by the blizzard. "Good eating," she whispered.

I should have followed. As Chooser, I should have abandoned the warmth and ease of the human's shelter, but the simple truth is I couldn't. The journey had drained me. I had nothing left. I collapsed in the dusty warmth of the human's roost, clinging to the broad flat perch, panting. If that roost had caught fire and burned to the ground, I couldn't have moved. Within moments, I slipped into a deep, deep sleep.

It was a mixed blessing, to sleep so soundly and to wake in a strange place, disoriented, afraid for the Family.

I will say this — it was nothing short of miraculous finding refuge in this human structure. Though the wind blew relentlessly, and time and again we heard it tear at the walls, inside it remained as warm as a spring day. Snow melted in small puddles everywhere. Feathers began to regain their sheen. The human had returned and set down a black shiny square-shaped thing in the corner of the roost. After the human had pulled the thing's tail and stuck one end in a small hole in the wall, it begin to heave and whir. Long flat strips deep within the box began to glow an angry red — and then, suddenly, it began to blow warm air from its wide, dark mouth.

It grew easier to swallow once again as our throats, frozen and wind-scoured, returned to normal. By the time the human came back, the flock had recovered enough to demonstrate some spirit. Many stirred and protested, some fluttered to the enclosure's topmost wooden limb, and shouted. The human ignored our protests, crouched and placed two flat stones on the floor: one piled high with meat, fruit and other salvage, and one with water collected in an oval dimple in its center. The human seemed to have some kind of odd concern for the glowing black box. Before it left, it knelt in front of it, dragged it closer to the entrance, then wedged a branch in the roost's opening that prevented the flat wooden barrier from swinging completely shut.

"You see," Kym said, turning to me and indicating the departing human, "some of them aren't so bad."

I watched the human trudge away. "I don't even want to think about the amount of time we'll have to spend in prayer and purification after this. What," I asked, "did you say to it?"

"I asked for help," she answered. "… I think."

"Well, by the Maker," I said, "that was the most extraordinary thing. It's the first time I've ever seen a Crow and a human *talk*. And it couldn't have happened at a better time."

I approached the fruit with caution, lifted a piece of apple in my beak, swallowed it, then washed it back with water. I didn't feel any different, except of course less hungry and thirsty. I snatched another piece up and, when it didn't seem to have any ill effect on me, gave the Call to come and eat.

When everyone had eaten and I began to feel somewhat recovered, I looked out through the clear stone set in a wall of the roost. The snow continued as if it might never stop.

I turned to Kym. "I hate to ask more of you, but I must. Will you take charge in my absence?"

"Surely you're not still thinking of leaving?"

"I gave my word."

"Uncle, I'll accept the position if you insist, but I would much rather you stayed. I know you feel duty bound, but you are our Chooser. We've already lost several elders tonight. You have a special responsibility to take care of yourself."

"There are too many for Kyp to look after. Most of the Family followed him. I have to know they're all right."

She looked me directly in the eyes. "What good will it do the Kinaar if we lose you too?"

"Kym, I *chose* this. I *chose* to allow the Family to split. I have to find the others. It's our only hope to keep the Kinaar together after the storm."

Seeing that I wouldn't be deterred, Kym laid her head on my shoulder and placed her beak against my neck. "The wind under your wings, Uncle," she whispered. "Good eating at the other end."

"Good eating, Niece." I spread my wings and tested them. "This was a fine thing you did. Now, keep watch over my Family. Make sure everyone comes to a safe roost when I see you next."

CHAPTER 22

Steam and mist coiled off the stream, transforming the tunnel into something spectral. In the drifting fog, ghostly shapes seemed to hover, then disappear. The tunnel walls shimmered under a fine, glittering layer of ice, making walking treacherous. One Crow would slip and several others would stumble over the prone body. Winding through the center of the tunnel, the stream — grown somewhat larger from the recent addition of rain and snow — meandered. Whenever a Crow fell into it, it was with shock that they found it warm to the touch. That warmth provided some small measure of hope, and in that dark, enclosed place, any hope was welcome.

At last, Kyp called for a halt. There was a slight bump as

each Crow settled into place, then a quiet fell, broken only by the occasional low moan of wind and the rhythmic panting of Crows. Every few breaths, the humans' lights above ground would flare and cast a beam through one of the grated holes above.

For all that they were cramped, frightened and disoriented, they were already much warmer. Though the wind whistled through the tunnel, it was a diminished version of the tempest that bent trees double above ground. The water that sprang from the crack steamed. As it flowed through the tunnel, it raised the temperature slightly, and the press of wing against wing warmed things as well.

Had everything gone well, that might be how the night was remembered — an awkward, sleepless, uncomfortable roost spent crushed one against the other. Our Family might have passed the night and come out the following morning grumbling and tired, but safe.

But it was as they rested that the first cat struck.

CHAPTER 23

I left the human shelter and the wind set on me. Everywhere, the tortured air whined and howled. Just *seeing* became a challenge. Snow caked around my eyes and crusted on my beak. Flight required the use of all my other senses, but each was diminished by the storm as well.

I have never experienced such difficulty flying. Exhausted already from the previous flights, each stroke of my wings was measured by a corresponding dull ache in my shoulders. Where my body didn't throb, it was numb.

Before long, my head began to swim and I realized I was completely lost in a heaving sea of white and black. There was no up or down, no forward or back. Suddenly a branch sprang out and raked my face, stinging and waking me, even as I tumbled through a dense thicket of young willow. I lay in the snow where I had been dumped and glanced about — I had flown into a tree, completely unaware.

I began to understand that if I didn't pull myself together at once and concentrate, I wouldn't survive. I blinked and spied a small hollow at the base of the willow carved out of the snow by the wind. I dragged myself into the shelter and was at last able to catch my breath. The numbness gradually disappeared from my face and back. As my senses returned, I felt something sharp poke my right shoulder. I turned and to my horror faced a gaping mouth sprouting a set of enormous jagged teeth.

Half buried in the snow and branches, the frozen features of a blood-spattered coyote stared defiantly. Injured, it must have sought shelter in the hollow and then died. As the temperature dropped, it had frozen, its lips curled in pain and rage. Now it was stiff and as solid as the stone-cold branches it sheltered beneath. I considered its grisly death mask and then, shaken, flew on.

Following Kyp's instructions, I at last came upon the ravine, where I searched through the brush and branches along the riverbank for the entrance. I spied something that looked like one of our folk below — something dark dashed across my line of vision, down near the ground. But when I blinked, the image disappeared. I shook my head to dislodge the snow that had pasted itself to my beak. Then, all at once, there was the tunnel entrance in front of me. I folded my wings, stooped and came to rest on a fallen log.

No sooner had I set talon to log than I was struck from the side and knocked flat. If it hadn't been for the soft, full depth of that freshly fallen snow, I wouldn't be alive today. The cat had caught me on the ground and unawares and had sliced clean through the tip of my right wing. But the snow disadvantaged the cat. As I lay shaken on my side, it attempted to pounce, but its rear legs only thrust deeper into the sticky snow. I labored to rise and hopped under a branch.

Too slow. In an instant, the Striped was on me, crashing through the undergrowth, slashing at the twigs. It caught me a glancing blow on my chest and then lashed me across my already cut right wing. Had it taken its time and been more meticulous about its attack, I would have been its next meal. Instead, it thrust its face in close to maul me. Seizing my chance, I lunged and caught it with the point of my beak above its lip, just under the nose. In a fight, when you're given the advantage of surprise, you use it. I jabbed again and caught it on the left eye, drawing blood.

I knew I couldn't win. I'd done what damage I could, now I needed to escape. I flung myself backward into a gooseberry thicket, hoping that the thick crush of thorns would catch at the cat's fur and slow it down. The pain was intense. I leaped to a stump. I wasn't sure my injured wing would support my full weight, but I had to try. I threw my wings out, lifted off — and was immediately dragged back to earth. The cat broke through the brambles as though they were nothing and snagged me along my left flank with its right front paw, splaying me out flat against the snow. Its jagged claws bit into my side. Its enormous, shaggy, ice-crusted face pressed next to me, cavernous mouth thrown open, coarse red tongue extended, teeth glistening. The smell of its breath enveloped me, rank, sharp, rotten. I closed my eyes.

Suddenly, I heard the most horrible sound. A rasping, tearing, discordant note like nothing I have ever heard. I opened my eyes and saw the cat's mouth stretched wide in anguish. Its weight lifted off me, and the creature flung itself end over end through the snow.

Shouting like a mad thing, Kyrk was on and beneath the Striped at the same time. He must have landed full on the cat's back and used both talon and beak — deep cuts ran up and down the cat's neck, and its right ear was nearly torn away. I have both seen and been in fights, but nothing to approach this. Kyrk fought like a thing possessed. He seemed years younger, strong and agile. He kept the Striped off balance and struck again and again.

Then, out of the tunnel, the White darted — his collar jangling crazily under his throat as he charged across the snow at Kyrk. I shrieked at Kyrk to fly! He threw himself to the side, rolled in the air and was up. The White sprang late and missed, tumbling headfirst into the snow. I had just enough presence of mind to realize that the cats would turn on me next. I launched myself and gave several short, sharp thrusts at the air, my right wing shooting with pain each time. The White coiled, jumped and caught the tip of my tail feathers. A quick stab of pain, the sight of tail feathers drifting to the ground, and I was up and out of range.

I wasn't able to fly far, but I followed Kyrk to a small hollow knot in a gnarled old spruce. It couldn't be described as shelter really, but at least it provided some relief from the wind. I crowded in next to him and eased to my haunches.

"Are you all right?" he asked, his voice slurred.

I realized his tongue had been sliced — the tip was just dangling. I assured him that I was fine. He'd taken a terrible mauling. A huge cut ran under his neck from the lower corner of his beak right to the base of his belly.

Then suddenly it struck me. "There's another one," I said.

"What?" he asked.

"Another cat. Gone down the tunnel. I saw a flash of something when I flew over, but didn't register what it was. It's a black cat. If it attacks the flock along with those two others, in the dark …" I didn't have to finish. We both knew what three cats were capable of doing. In that place with nowhere for a Crow to fly — they could kill them all.

CHAPTER 24

The human returned once more and brought with it fresh water and some kind of crushed, mashed carcass, which it arranged in the stone on the floor.

After the human left, Kym hopped down beside the salvage. Because she was acting as Chooser, the Clan waited until she had tested it. It's difficult to judge by conventional methods what is fit to eat when it comes to human goods. So often Crows have judged something fit and then found themselves poisoned, that the best one can do is to sample a small portion and let time pass. (Although with human goods, it's hard to know how much time is necessary.) In any case, the Kemnas watched Kymmy test the food, and waited. Finally, when it seemed safe, she gave the Call. The flock descended from their perches and ate.

Suddenly Kym shuddered. "What is it?" Katy asked.

"I have a bad feeling," Kym replied.

"About the food?" Katy stopped in mid-swallow. "It *seems* good. I haven't tasted anything —"

"No, not the food. About the others." Kym turned her head as if listening or trying to recapture a memory. "Just now I felt a — I don't know what it was — a shiver, and I just *know* they're in some sort of trouble."

"What can you do?"

"I'm not sure," she said slowly, trying to work it through. "But I think … I think I'm going to go look for Kalum, just to make sure he made it away safely."

But at that precise moment, the wind rose and struck the piece of wood at the roost's entrance. It bounced once, hard, and the stick that had held it ajar suddenly popped up and spun out into the snow. The flat wood recoiled and came slapping back against the wall, snapping into place and barring the way. Though Kymmy tried and several others helped, there was nothing to be done. There was no way of getting out anymore. They were, all of them, trapped.

When it looked like the Clan might hurt itself trying to get under or through the wood blocking the opening, Kym told everyone to rest.

She settled on the floor by the now-barred opening. We're here for the night. That's all there is to it, she thought and tried, unsuccessfully, to put the rest of the Family out of her mind.

CHAPTER 25

There are newlings who believe that as you get older, you outgrow fear, or set it aside and replace it with courage, the way you replace a fledgling's downy feathers for the darker, stronger feathers of an adult. That's simply not true. As I stepped into the tunnel, I've never felt so sick-to-my-stomach scared. I shook, and if I didn't cry out, it was only because it took all my concentration not to turn around and fly out. Banged up as he was, though, Kyrk maintained a complete and utterly calm demeanor, and there were many times I relied upon that composure to steady me.

As the deeper darkness enveloped us and the tunnel walls closed around us, every story I had ever heard in the nest, every rumor I'd learned from my grandfather as I pecked for bugs by his side, rushed back to me. Underground was a place of death. It was the roost of spirits, the perch of the night falcon who hunts and haunts our nightmares.

I've said before that there's no shame in flying from a fight you can't win, and that's true. But let me say this: All of life is training, and for what? To fight a battle that can't be won, because eventually Death flies out of the night, unexpected, and plucks up each one of us. All our lives are training to prepare us for that last pitch and peck in the dark. If you can't face death, you cannot face life. As Kyrk and I walked, I had to keep reminding myself of that.

We moved cautiously, he and I, listening as we went. Stopping and resting. Listening again. Walking. In the flickering light, there were many times I felt certain I saw something, then as the light dimmed, concluded I hadn't. It was an especially difficult walk because we had to ignore our every instinct. We couldn't rush. The tunnel surface was uneven, and in the dark we risked tripping and making noise. We couldn't call out. Our only hope of providing help was through surprise. All we could do was move forward, one cautious step after another. Listen after each step. And pray.

As we rounded one turn, the light flared blue white, and in that brief instant I saw the tunnel curling ahead of us like the vast shimmering gullet of an enormous coiling snake — the stream winding down the center, mist rising above it, the icy sheen glittering off the walls like scales.

Then the light winked out and I felt rather than heard a flurry of movement. A sharp stab of pain jolted me as a paw glanced off my already-hurt right wing. Another blow caught me on the lower end of my spine, snapping my head back, throwing me down. As I scrambled to rise, I heard the shrill yowl of a cat mixed with Kyrk's harsh curses as they tumbled over each other in the dark. Then all at once, I sensed a new presence. A quick flurry of wings, another Crow's voice, and the cat began to scream. That scream echoed up and down the tunnel, then abruptly halted. Silence fell.

The light flickered once more, and there, in that flare of illumination, I saw Kuper, his feathers standing all askew, his beak open, panting. Beside and slightly behind him crouched Kyrk, and at their talons, flat and still, the limp form of a dead cat. The light winked out again.

Had the Great Crow himself been standing before me in all his glory, I could not have been more amazed. "How, in the name of the Maker," I asked Kuper, "did *you* get here?"

"I had to stop and rest on my way through the ravine. At the top of the rise, I saw a cat slip through a hole dug under a stone grid and figured that since it was close to the tunnel, it must somehow be connected. The cat scampered on ahead, and I kept after it. I'd only arrived at the first fork when I heard a noise down this way. I came up behind this one, and you."

Kyrk suddenly spoke from beside me in the darkness.

"This isn't one of the cats that attacked us outside," he rasped hoarsely.

That took me aback. "Are you certain?"

"Positive." And as he said that, the lights flickered up and, sure enough, there lay the Tan. "So there are at least three more in here, somewhere."

"Three?" Kuper repeated with alarm. I quickly filled him in on what had happened. He released a string of curses, then asked, "Do we know where the rest of the Family is?"

"They have to be farther down the tunnel."

Kuper peered ahead. "Have you heard anything from them?"

"Nothing." I replied.

Kyrk was already suffering from cuts he had received in the struggle outside the tunnel entrance, as well as bruises and cuts from the Tan. And Kuper had barely recovered his breath from his flight or this most recent skirmish, yet neither of them hesitated. Kyrk stretched his wings. "Are you ready?" he asked Kuper.

"Yes," Kuper replied.

Kuper turned to me. "You?"

I was limping, but of the three of us, I believe I was the least injured. "Ready as I'll ever be."

Kyrk struggled to his talons. "Then we'd better get going."

The words had only barely left his beak when we heard a new clamor down the tunnel. Crows and cats in deadly struggle.

CHAPTER 26

Here was the situation: Eight hundred of the Family pressed underground in unimaginably confined conditions. Effectively blind. No light except for the occasional dim flickering through grates farther up and down the tunnel. The only one who knew his way in or out with certainty, Kyp. Eight hundred Crows, pressed wing to wing, in the deepest, darkest dark, with nothing but the breath of the bird next to them and the smell of fear to keep them company.

That's the way things were when the Red hit.

As far as we can tell, the first few had no chance, the killing began that quietly. Kolf, Kypa, Krak and Kerda, Kaif and Kaifa, Kuru, Kark and Kralak dropped silent as dust. By my calculations, at least twelve individuals had fallen before Klayton heard something, felt a rush of wind and had the presence of mind to peck first and ask questions later. He's a strong bird, thick-necked and quick. When his beak struck fur, fast as lightning he lunged again. The Red released a horrifying warbling howl, bursting with pain and hatred. That's when the panic hit.

To kill something to eat is natural. We Crows do that. Sometimes we kill to defend ourselves. But there is something perverse, a sickness or madness that occurs only among humans and their slaves. I've seen humans kill other humans and discard their bodies to litter the earth. I've seen dogs rage among penned rabbits, grasp one, shake it, snap its neck and move to the next — not stopping to feed, nor bury for later use, but simply satisfying a kind of killing lust. Something of this must have been upon the Red.

With no order or discipline in place among our folk, the Red might have carried on undeterred. For this reason, our greatest danger lay in that initial moment of panic. A terrible noise followed the Red's cry as everywhere wings beat — and then immediately after, the sound of bodies striking stone filled the tunnel. Crows hurled themselves against the walls and were crushed as other Crows hurtled against them. Groans, pleas for help, cries of confusion and terror and pain rose in a deafening uproar — and no one knew where to go or what to do. Talons stretched and clutched as Crow clambered over Crow. Suddenly, a great rush of our folk swept for the lower entrance, only to find themselves penned in and attacked by yet another cat.

Had the Family continued in this fashion, it's not certain even one Crow would have escaped. In the turmoil, we Crows might have done terrible damage to ourselves, and then the cats, endowed as they were with better vision, hearing and traction, could have finished their work at leisure.

Instead, Kyp cried out over top of all that clamor and chaos. He pleaded for calm. He urged folk at the perimeter to assist one another, and when the cats next struck, they were met with beaks and wings and talons. Startled and hurt, the cats fell back. In that pause, Kyp reorganized the flock. He moved the strongest and fittest to the outer edge. He matched each Crow with a partner and had the team stand back to back. I'm not sure that this made a great difference tactically, but what it did for the flock's spirit was immeasurable. To know that there was a plan, to know that no one need face the cats alone — this helped more than anything else might have.

The cats retreated hurt, but they didn't retreat far. The hurt they'd received wasn't enough to stop them, but it was more than enough to make them very, very angry. When they returned, they hoped to surprise our Family once again, but those on the perimeter were ready, and the cats met an even stiffer resistance. Again they withdrew. When they returned next, they came silently in pairs attacking from the front and rear.

So one Crow would fall. Two others would crowd in to take his place. The cats would retire and search for another place to attack. It was a longer game, but still one in deadly earnest. That is what we came upon, Kyrk, Kuper and I.

So immersed were the cats in their sport that they never imagined other Crows might join late. When Kyrk and I fell on one, his surprise was considerable. Caught from behind, he wasn't prepared to fight on two fronts and fled immediately. Kuper leaped into the conflict on our left. As luck would have it, his first strike struck the cat on the cheek and his beak withdrew a clump of fur and whiskers. The cat yowled and ran right over the top of Kuper in his escape.

After the shrill noise of cat squalls and Crow curses, a strange quiet descended upon the tunnel. "Does anyone know exactly how many cats we're dealing with?" I shouted.

Kyp sounded as composed as if he was directing me to the nearest bugs or berries.

"Kalum? Four, as far as I can tell. Two initially, and two arrived recently. We've been fighting them at each end of the tunnel. When did you get here?"

"Just now. Kyrk is with me, and Kuper."

I winced as I stumbled over something large and soft and felt feathers between my talons. One of our fallen relatives.

"Kyp?" I called, "how bad is it?"

"We were hurt most in the first attack. Once we got organized, we held our own. So you know, one of these four is the Red."

"The Red?" Kuper's voice sounded grim. "Maybe I can collect the rest of his tail."

I felt time pressing. How soon could we expect the next attack? "Kyp?"

"Yes?"

"What's the best route to get back to the surface?"

"The way we came in. It's the most direct."

"Where are the cats likely to be now?"

"They've shifted up the tunnel, perhaps down a side shaft. Not far, I'd guess."

"Then we'll have to fight our way out."

"I expect so."

We held a brief conference, Kyp, Kyrk, Kuper and myself. We quickly rearranged our largest and strongest adults at the rear and front of the flock, in two separate units — one to take the first fight with the cats, and one group to hop up and glide low over the top. We took a quick tally of the wounded, placed them and the young at the center and began to move back toward the tunnel's mouth.

But, oh, it was a slow pace. Walking has never been a movement best suited to Crows, and certainly not after nearly a day of flying and fighting. Our legs ached from continuous tension as much as anything else, and almost half of our folk in that tunnel had already taken an injury. So we walked and rested, and when we were able to move again, on we went.

What the cats didn't know, and what no outsider can understand, is the ability of the Family to pull together as a group when called upon. An eternity of migrating back and forth has endowed us with the skill — when there's the need — to take order instantly.

So when the Red and his bunch did attack again, what did they meet? Not Crows caught unawares. When the Red slashed out, he caught the breasts of Kaitlen and Kekko, but in an instant, five beaks flashed forward just as quickly. If even one beak made contact, the Red must have been hurt badly. And as soon as the second line heard the attack, they leaped over the front line, clawing the backs and necks of whatever cat they landed upon.

That's how it went for what seemed like an eternity — we Crows retreating painfully, one faltering step after another. Every few moments fending off another of the cats' slashing attacks. One Crow would fall, and Kyp would have another take his place.

At one point, the cats attacked simultaneously from both sides, as well as from above. A ledge of some sort must have provided a cat with the opportunity to perch and silently wait for us. For a time, there was a very real danger that our defense would collapse. Despite our best preparations, many of our strongest, fittest Crows lost their lives. Keer and Kulemna fell when a cat landed on their unprotected backs from above. Some of the Crows in the middle, fearful of a rout, began to panic and crowd. Kyp and Kuper were everywhere, calming those who were rattled, moving injured Crows aside, pecking and clawing and fighting and shouting encouragement. Kuper struggled his way to the center, caught the cat that was mauling the flock and drove him back up a side shaft.

It was just after we had repelled this last attack, and I didn't know if I had the strength to lift my head or wings again. I was resting next to Kyp, trying to catch my breath, when suddenly one could sense something shift. The Family had maintained its movement toward the main entrance despite the cats' best efforts. Our resolve had been tested, but never seriously faltered.

Cut and bruised, discerning that the battle was no longer going their way, the cats began to reconsider things. I heard the sound of soft footpads, and as the light flickered, I briefly spied something slinking up a side tunnel. "Don't let it get away!" Kuper shouted and raced off in pursuit. Others might have joined that chase, but at that same moment, a great commotion arose at the opposite end of the tunnel. The Striped had apparently attempted a quick snatch and run, then had experienced a change of heart and simply fled. Twenty or so Crows gave immediate chase. The Striped sped through the tunnels as quickly as he could with the Family following closely, until at last he found himself outside, surrounded by snow and storm.

If the wind had proved a hindrance to our flight, now the deep snow proved an equal problem for the Striped. Chest deep, struggling to free his paws, he found himself in a completely exposed position with an angry Mob close behind. He turned to escape into a thicket where he might at least hope to split the attack among the bramble and brush but, as I've said, in a race of wings against legs, bet on wings. The first Crows struck his hindquarters and knocked him off balance. The Striped opened his mouth to yowl, but the driving wind swallowed his cries and the Mob was on him. The fight was bitter but brief. The Mob made short work of him and then returned to the tunnel's mouth.

In the meantime, Kuper continued to pursue the cat he had spied. What I hadn't been able to see that Kuper's keener eyes had was the White retreating with Kelta draped from his jaws. Unwilling to let the White escape with his prize, Kuper performed a quick calculation. Judging from where he had last spotted the cat, he leaped through the dark, catching the White's right hind leg. Startled, the big cat snarled, releasing Kelta. She scrambled out of the way as Kuper and the White tangled in a jumble of fur and feathers.

At another time and place, the White might have stayed to finish the kill, but realizing that he had lost his first meal and that Kuper seemed unwilling to provide him with another, panic descended upon the cat. The White batted Kuper against the wall, then turned and fled. Kuper picked himself off the floor and flew in pursuit. Kelta called after Kuper to let the White go or await help, but Kuper was possessed.

The White had traveled only a short distance when again he felt pain shoot up his rear leg — Kuper. He turned and attacked with purpose. He threw three rapid blows to Kuper's head, then hesitated as he felt a cut open over his brow and blood filled his eyes. In a rage, he pounced and trampled Kuper, then hearing others approaching, turned again and fled. Only at the tunnel's entrance did he discover he could no longer see. Kuper's slash had cut clean across the cat's eyes.

The side entrance the White had selected opened upon

the crest of a limestone shelf. Even without the use of his eyes, the cat could sense the ground falling away suddenly at his feet, and he shrank back from the edge. In that moment of hesitation, Kuper caught up. Too crippled to fly anymore, but stubbornly refusing to give up, he had glided, hopped and now flung himself through the air in an extended dive. He struck the White in his generous midsection, just beneath the rib cage. The White was blinded but could still smell and hear. He turned, swept at Kuper with one paw and made contact. Sharp claws penetrated deep into the muscle tissue of Kuper's left shoulder. The White yanked Kuper closer, lunged and grasped him between his jaws.

In a frenzy of frustration and anger, he reared full up on its hind legs, clamped his jaws tight and, with a bone-snapping toss of his head, shook Kuper. The lip of snow beneath his hind paws fractured and collapsed. Down the steep escarpment they fell, ricocheting off rock outcroppings, rolling and finally landing with a muffled, sickening crack against the base of a hoary old spruce. When Kelta finally crawled to the entranceway, she saw them below — nestled together as though sleeping, quietly gathering snow.

Back in the tunnel, the tone of the battle had changed. It was no longer we Crows who were on the defensive, but the cats. Every Crow flew to wherever they heard a commotion and looked to assist. The struggle pushed on up the tunnel, and when it became clear that the two remaining cats were now just trying to escape, the Family increased their efforts. Fearing that the cats would double back, Kyp called to the flock to stay together. But as he shouted, he felt a sharp blow from behind, and darkness took him.

CHAPTER 27

Kyp's head throbbed. His throat was parched, and he felt both dizzy and disoriented. He knew only one thing for certain — that he was rocking gently from side to side in a completely unfamiliar manner. For the life of him, he was unable to understand how he came to be moving at all. His wings appeared to be pinned tightly at his sides. His legs were at rest as well. It was only as he grew more alert that he understood his situation: he was clamped in a cat's jaws, his wings wedged between its sharp teeth. With horror, he realized he was being carried to a private place where the cat could devour him undisturbed.

Once the struggle had turned and the Black had fled, the Red had resolved to settle his score with Kyp before slipping away. He knew Kyp's scent and the sound of his voice — no one better. When he heard Kyp shout, he had swatted him, then gathered him up. Not wanting to have his dinner interrupted, the Red hadn't taken the time to kill the unconscious Kyp, but had silently padded away.

As Kyp rocked back and forth in the darkness, he realized that he would have to make his move quickly. The sounds of the flock were already fading. Unless Kyp could free himself, the Red need do nothing more than draw his jaws shut. Kyp glanced about in that gloom and realized that the Red had carried him back to the spot where the flock had rested. Above and to his left, the hot spring emerged and dribbled down the wall from the dark fracture. The Red clearly meant to thaw himself and dine.

Kyp craned his neck about and struck, catching the cat full on the sensitive inner flap of his nose. The Red shrieked in pain and instinctively released his grip on Kyp, who pushed free and unfurled his wings. He sailed out of the cat's mouth — and promptly struck the roof of the tunnel. The Red made a desperate lunge. Kyp swiftly swung to his right, away from the swiping paws. Again he ricocheted off the walls, bruising an already-injured right shoulder.

In the tunnel's confines, unable to see properly or fly fully, Kyp understood that it was only a matter of time until the Red snagged him. Once knocked to the floor, he'd be helpless.

Instead, Kyp darted for the crack in the wall. He hesitated only a moment, then slipped into the dark, damp enveloping warmth. He had no idea how far back the cavern coiled, if there was another exit or how to find it if there was, but he could sense the immensity of the space stretching far into the distance. He limped up the slippery rock to a stony outcrop and stood panting, neck cut, wing cut, bone tired. Moments later, the air shifted and Kyp sensed another presence enter: the Red.

Now, the Red hadn't escaped injury. A gash ran up and along his face from the soft fleshy nose almost to one eye, impairing his ability to smell. On his right front paw, one claw had been completely removed. There were still a number of cuts only barely healed from his previous encounter with the Mob. But his anger was intact, coursing through him cold and pure and fierce, and it drove him on. Slowly he crept forward, testing the air, listening. Listening for an intake of breath, for a scrape of talon against rock — and each time he heard a noise, he lifted a pad and moved another step closer to Kyp.

Slowly, so slowly it strained each bruised muscle, Kyp probed the ground around him with the tip of his beak. At last he found a pebble of a suitable size. He clasped the pebble tightly between his upper and lower beak and cautiously lifted it. With a quick, clean flick of his head, he flung the pebble to the right. The pebble clattered across a rocky surface. Instantly, the Red sprinted in that direction, almost tumbling into a cleft that opened at his feet. Kyp heard the Red's claws scrabble against the slick cave floor.

Cat and Crow froze now and took stock in that thick, cloying darkness. Barely breathing. Poised. Ready.

Then Kyp made a decision.

Bats can fly in complete darkness. We Crows pride ourselves on our ability to fly by instinct, but still require some light to maneuver by, even if it's only starlight. And as developed as their night vision and their senses of smell and hearing are, cats still need some light to operate by, too. Kyp knew that the Red held the advantage as soon as there was the slightest flicker of light. But in total darkness, as long as Kyp had the use of his wings and didn't crash into any rock outcropping, he had the advantage of mobility. So now Kyp summoned all the skill he had developed in a lifetime of flying and lifted off. He flew in tight, controlled circles, trying to remain absolutely level, knowing if he raised a single feather too much one way, or lowered a wing too much another, he'd strike a rock — and the game would be over.

The Red cocked his head. Sensed the rush of air and the stroke of wings just above him. Waited for the lights to flicker on.

Kyp glanced off a rocky outcrop and grunted with pain. Suddenly he heard the clatter of loose pebbles as the Red rushed toward the sound. At once Kyp pivoted and dropped, striking the Red hard with his shoulder. The Red spun, lunged and caught Kyp with the tips of his claws — not a serious cut, but the slash cast Kyp reeling against an upraised spire. Somewhere, the lights crackled and blinked, and in that moment, the Red spied Kyp prone on the glittering rock escarpment. He leaped just as the lights winked out again, but when he landed, Kyp had rolled to the side. In that instant, as his paws struck the water-polished rock, the Red lost his footing. A great cry filled the cavern, and then the sickening sound of claws scraping against hard rock, followed by the clatter and echo of something falling a long way down.

The lights winked on for an instant, glinting off ripples spreading across the glossy surface of a pool far down at the bottom of the cavern. Kyp turned away. When next the lights winked on, he tiredly limped through the crevice and back into the tunnel.

CHAPTER 28

That marked the end of that struggle and a night of heartache and loss. The storm gradually blew itself out. By mid-evening, the wind had dropped and only the lightest snow continued to fall. There were many, many wounded to take care of. Individuals were appointed to groom the injured and carry them beakfuls of water. Only after I had attended to the sick and wounded did I get an opportunity to search for Kyrk.

I found him on the floor not far from the tunnel's main entrance. He was bloodied from head to talon, a long, ugly gash running from his good right eye down his neck and through his breast.

"So?" he asked, his voice hoarse and thick.

I crouched beside him. "The Red has been taken care of."

"Excellent," he croaked, closing his eyes. Moments later, he opened them again. "Who was responsible?"

"Kyp."

"Good for him," he said and nodded with some satisfaction, but a slight shudder ran the length of his body. His beak gaped and he panted as if returning from a long, hard flight. He fought to keep his good eye on me.

"I have something to tell you. I erred. I was to perform backup, but I couldn't face going underground. I thought it would be sufficient to guide the flock in and keep watch above ground, but the cold and wind caused me to nod off. I woke only when I heard your cries. Tell Kyp he did well. Tell him he was right. He's smart, smarter than I ever gave him credit for, but he needs to think things through, and he needs to consult. Tell him that. He should run his decisions by that other young one, Kym." Another shudder ran through his body.

"What are you talking about?" I asked.

Kyrk focused his good eye on me — no one has ever given me such a penetrating look. "When he becomes Chooser, of course. You still probably have a few years left — if you watch what you eat and get more exercise. But you can't expect to stay on forever."

"You'll be able to remind me of that for some time yet."

"No," he said and coughed. "I'm done. You've been a good Chooser."

"I didn't see this coming."

Kyrk shook his head. "No one saw this coming. It's not seeing what's coming that makes a good Chooser. It's being able to handle what comes unseen. You passed. I failed."

"You didn't fail, Kyrk."

"You think?" he asked and coughed again. "Well, maybe. Not entirely. In any case, I fly ahead. This time I leave it to you to perform backup." And with that he laid his craggy head down and closed his eyes. He always was a Crow of few words.

Not since the passing of my wife, Karla, has any death affected me so profoundly. Kyrk was my elder. I knew him from the time I was an egg. He was canny and resourceful, and for most of my life I relied on him for advice. In later years, he grew tired and bitter, and out of that tiredness and bitterness he sometimes made mistakes. He would speak harshly without cause. He could be petty and vindictive. But he never ever stopped loving the Family. And his death was as brave and honorable a death as ever I've seen. I will remember him in the quiet of my thoughts for that, and for all the other many good deeds he has done me and the Family. With Kyrk's death, we experience a huge loss.

The remainder of the night was spent resting in the tunnel. We had earned our right to stay. The cut and wounded tended their injuries as best they could. Each bird pressed up next to the other for warmth and groomed one another. Still, many of the most badly wounded perished before dawn.

Finally, day broke, the clouds scattered and the sun rose. As the rays touched the landscape, one could at last gather the full impact of the storm's violence. Wherever one turned, the desolation was nearly complete. It was as if an immense wing had swept over the entire land. Enormous knots of branches and broken tree trunks lay in tangled heaps at ground level. Snow layered everything five or six Crows high. Where it had drifted, it was ten, maybe twelve Crows high. Birds of all kinds lay stiff on the ground or crouched frozen, still attached under ice and snow to the perch where they had spent the night, trying to escape the blizzard.

Kyp landed next to me, but it was several moments before I could draw my eyes away from that appalling scene.

"Uncle," he began in a low voice.

"Yes?"

"I wish to pass Choosing back to you."

"Yes. Of course. And thank you."

"I will continue to help in whatever way I can, in whatever way is most useful to the Kinaar, but I will understand once things have settled, when you convene the Family and Banish me."

"Banish you?" I turned to him, but he was staring straight ahead. "For what?"

"For leading the Family into danger. For negligence. For thinking I was able to do something I couldn't. For failure."

"I see."

"I understand that Kyrk has made the trip." Kyp hadn't phrased that as a question, but it was, and I nodded my reply. "Well. He would be satisfied, if he were here, to confirm just how right he was about me."

"Do you think?" I asked, then told him Kyrk's final words.

"But he was right! The tunnel proved deadly. We were attacked, just as he'd feared. We lost Crows. So many hurt, so many —" His voice broke.

"Listen to me," I said. "Last night *every* choice was bad. You fought hard to protect the Family. You returned the flock to my care, and you have nothing to be ashamed of. Yes, Crows died. But look about you. Would any of us have survived the night above ground? You did everything you could. I won't be calling for a judgment."

"But —"

I flapped a wing at him. "You feel disappointed? Good. And hurt, and small, and capable of error? Good. Live with it. Remember that feeling. When you're faced with another difficult choice, let it temper your judgment. Now, Nephew," I said, looking at the wreckage left in the storm's wake, "we have many other things to concern ourselves with this day. It's best if we get going."

I gave the Call and we lifted into the sky, wheeled about once and set out for the Gathering Tree.

CHAPTER 29

Kym slept a dreamless sleep, fatigued beyond measure. She awoke with a start, sensing a shift in the air. She opened her eyes, blinked and saw the human. Scrambling to her talons, she tried to shake off her weariness. How had it entered the roost without alarming anyone? The human stepped closer and Kym stiffened. Slowly it crouched and stretched a hairy limb in her direction. She fought the impulse to fly to a higher perch and avoid its touch. It uncurled a massive paw, revealing five blunt, pink fleshy claws. Gently it touched Kym and stroked her beneath the beak and along her throat, its claws' rounded tips surprisingly delicate. Then the human stood, reached out and pushed aside the wooden slat barring the entrance.

The first rays of the sunrise spilled in, gold and red. Outside, the snow lay in great sweeping, perfect drifts, clean, sharp-edged and beautiful. The wind had dropped, and though it was still cold, one could feel that the storm had truly broken. Kym called to the others to awake and rise.

Crows raised their heads and stretched their wings. With a great rush, Kym swept past the human, and Crow after Crow followed, swung into the sky and then spiraled — higher, and then again higher still. The human could be seen below, small and frail seeming, stretching one thin limb and pink talon up above its head in a curious gesture of farewell.

CHAPTER 30

No one was prepared for what we saw when we arrived. There was our Gathering Tree, our protection, our shelter, our meeting place since before we were born, laid out on its side. It had not merely been snapped mid-trunk, as most other trees had. It was completely sundered, from the ground up, as though lightning-blasted. White and yellow shards lay scattered across the snow. Gnarled roots projected out of the earth. The tree that had sheltered me since I was a youth. The tree from which I had learned to fly. The tree I had perched upon, where I had listened to stories late into the night at so many Gatherings. Broken and lifeless.

I know that no one place is special to the Maker, for all places are special to her, yet some places help us to see the Maker more clearly. That was what the Gathering Tree did for me. I felt the Maker most closely when I was in that tree, and with its ruin I felt as lost as I have ever felt.

I'm afraid that was how Kym found me when she returned to the Gathering Tree. She said nothing, but came directly to my side and rested her head upon my shoulder. Kyp limped along the branch, and asked how many had returned with her. It was then, perched amid the scattered ruins of our old Gathering Tree, that I learned the full extent of our loss. All those who had fallen in our battles with cats and the elements.

As you know, it is our way not to count any as dead until their death can be formally recognized before the Family. Now the time has come to perform this rite.

Listen, all. In that evening of the Storm, between killing cold and the claws of cats, we lost Kyrk, and Kuper, Kork, Kaleb, Keir, Kerda, Kark, KuKulan, Kester and Kyf, Ketch and Ketch the younger, Kyt and Koso, Ketta and Keera, all of the Korin line: Kory, Korreta, Koreen and Koran. Kynata, who was the oldest of her line, Kypa, Kufa, Kufeela, Kupella, Kulemna; Kolf, Kaifa, Kaira, Kaita, Kaif and Kuru; Keela and her four sons, Keer, Keeru, Keeratin and Keefar. Kakyna and all his line: Kakaryna, Kakatar, Kakafar, Kapella, Koona and Kooso. The four sisters: Karu, Kapu, Katu, and Kwys. Krak, Kralak, Kretch, Kram, Kruppa, Krail, Kent and Kaneeta, Kora and Kold. Kelm and Keeta survived the night but died of wounds in the morning, as did Kylly, Kyd, Kona, Kifi, Kood, Kalf, Kalfa, Kles, Kyrr and Kyrreta, Kartu and Kellar. All in all, seventy-two souls returned to the Maker that night.

Our ways are clear. Out of respect, these names will be retired for the passing of a full cycle. We will remember the qualities of those who have left us. Each time we recall these names, we will remember the strengths these Crows possessed, and when finally we restore these honored titles and endow featherless nestlings with them, it will not be with grief, for the wind will have cleansed us, and time will have healed us, and grief will have flown from our hearts. What will remain will be pride. What will remain will be devotion. What will remain will be respect for the sacrifices these individuals made on our behalf. Listen. The Maker calls them now.

They are gone. Their souls have left us. May the Maker support us.

Join me in a moment of silence.

As I told you, when I returned to our Gathering Tree I couldn't help but wonder what would happen to us. I perched on that massive trunk lying prone in the snow and let my spirit roam with the Maker. The sun had risen higher in the sky, and water had begun to gather on every branch. I heard it slip from the tips of the emerging leaves and fall to the soft snow in a thousand tiny musical drops. Humans began to emerge from their shelters. On their broad, flat faces one could see reflected emotions similar to ours: Shock. Dismay. Discouragement. Sadness. Some cleared the snow from in front of their roosts. Some clambered to the top and pushed snow to the ground. Newling humans left their dens and began rolling in the snow, not unlike our own newlings.

There are so very many of them. Every time I look about, there are more. Humans prosper, but what of us Crows? What is to become of us? I cannot tell. This much is certain, though. Even from First Times there has been something intertwined in the destiny of Crows and humans. It will be up to this next generation to decipher this destiny and chart a new direction, and it will require strength, imagination and all our collective wisdom.

I looked down at our Gathering Tree and felt sorry for it — but as I looked, something caught my eye. Amid all that snow and water and debris, between two massive branches wedged in a snowdrift, something glittered like a single teardrop. I hopped down and plucked the glittering thing up — a solitary delicate freshwater pearl, as smooth and perfect as the first-formed dewdrop of the first spring, white as the downy feathers on the breast of a gull chick. Klara's offering from long ago.

It was at that moment that Kyp approached and told me of a new tree, farther down the valley of the beaver pond — an immense spreading willow that had withstood snow and wind, which had bent, but not broken.

I took this as a sign.

We flew here together, and as I perched among this tree's massive spreading limbs, I could feel running beneath my talons, under the bark, a supple, resilient and enduring strength.

Kyp is right. It is a good tree. I convened the remaining elders of our Family, consulted, and they agree. It's true that we have not performed the search as we have in the past, and perhaps tradition hasn't been followed. But perhaps it can be said that this tree has sought us out. Maybe that makes it all the more ours. Into this tree I have placed the pearl, this gift we received from the Maker, to consecrate it. May our new Gathering Tree bless us as the previous Gathering Tree blessed us for so very, very long.

This brings us to the end of the Telling. We have talked through the night and into the first faint glimmerings of day. By the light of this new dawn, I declare that you are all witnesses, and with witnessing comes responsibility. You know the full extent of the losses we experienced and the changes that have resulted. Among you are those farsighted enough to understand that there will be many more changes ahead. Humans will have an increasing role, and how we will deal with them is unclear to me. Long experience has taught us to be cautious in our dealings with humans, but in these recent events, curiously, we have benefited not only from human shelter but, impossible as it might seem, from human kindness.

There is a single final judgment to be rendered, and as Chooser, I alone can make it. Of all the deaths that occurred in the past few days, there are none I regret or feel more responsible for than those that befell our cousins as they sought refuge in the obstructed human shelter. Of all the fatalities, only those were avoidable. They resulted from impulsive, wrongheaded decision making. Had we stayed together, had we pooled our strengths, had I overruled Kork and not permitted that tragic Splitting, we would have been stronger in our struggle with the cats, and lives would not have been wasted seeking shelter that didn't exist. The flock was fortunate in that Kym salvaged what otherwise would have been a complete and crushing disaster, but the Family is too important to rely upon chance.

And that brings me to my last, and your first, decision of a new era. I am wise enough to know that the corner we are turning requires more ability and agility than this old mind possesses, and I put you all on notice. When we return next year to this Gathering Tree, you will select a new Chooser to lead the Family.

I realize this uncertainty causes some uneasiness. But remember, the Maker created light and life from darkness, and in the midst of all this ruination, she has sent us this extraordinary new tree as a sign that she has not forgotten us. It is up to us to grasp these past dark events and shape a new and brighter tomorrow from them.

Cousins, I cannot predict all the challenges we will encounter — their scale, their scope or their timing — but I can foretell this. We *will* survive them. We will survive them as we have survived the difficulties and challenges of the storm, the way Great Crow survived the darkness of Badger's den, the way our ancestors survived their many trials of the past. And because we are Crows, we will survive unlike any other creature on Earth. We will survive as only Crows can — with *style*.

We Crows find ourselves caught between earth and sky, between life as it was and life as it will be, between yesterday and tomorrow. Cousins, hear me, the wind has changed! It is no longer from the north, but blows clear

Acknowledgments

The Mob has been a considerable time in the making and there are a number of people I feel should be acknowledged.

I would like to thank my editor, Charis Wahl, and my agent, Janine Cheeseman, for their efforts and assistance. I should also thank all the people who read earlier drafts or offered thoughts and encouragement: Betty, Kate, Jason and John Poulsen; Catherine Barroll; Shayna and Kyle McNeil; Janet Lee-Evoy; Mary Ann Wilson and Brian Cooley; Alesha Porisky; Joanne Towers; Heather Baxter; Jennifer Baxter; Kirsten Strong; Laura Strong; Wendy Lunn; Diana Lunn; Jane Matheson; Rochelle Lamoureux; and the ever reliable Martinis, Olivier, Nic and my mother, Catherine Martini.

The Mob is the first in

THE CROW CHRONICLES

series, to be followed by

The Plague
and
The Judgment

Visit **www.thecrowchronicles.co.uk**
for more details